WORST CASE,
WE GET MARRIED

SOPHIE BIENVENU

TRANSLATED BY JC SUTCLIFFE

WORST CASE, WE GET MARRIED

Book*hug Press
Toronto, 2019
Literature in Translation Series

FIRST ENGLISH EDITION

Published originally in French under the title *Et au pire, on se mariera* by Les éditions La Mèche, an imprint of Groupe d'édition la courte échelle inc. Copyright © Les éditions La Mèche 2011

English translation copyright © 2019 by J.C. Sutcliffe

The production of this book was made possible through the generous assistance of the Canada Council for the Arts and the Ontario Arts Council. Book*hug Press also acknowledges the support of the Government of Canada through the Canada Book Fund and the Government of Ontario through the Ontario Book Publishing Tax Credit and the Ontario Book Fund.

We acknowledge the financial support of the Government of Canada through the National Translation Program for Book Publishing, an initiative of the Roadmap for Canada's Official Languages 2013-2019: Education, Immigration, Communities, for our translation activities.

Book*hug Press acknowledges the land on which it operates. For thousands of years it has been the traditional land of the Huron-Wendat, the Seneca, and most recently, the Mississaugas of the Credit River. Today, this meeting place is still the home to many Indigenous people from across Turtle Island, and we are grateful to have the opportunity to work on this land.

Library and Archives Canada Cataloguing in Publication

Title: Worst case, we get married / Sophie Bienvenu ; translated by J.C. Sutcliffe
Other titles: Et au pire, on se mariera. English
Names: Bienvenu, Sophie, 1980– author. | Sutcliffe, J. C., translator.
Series: Literature in translation series.
Description: First English edition. | Series statement: Literature in translation series | Translation of: Et au pire, on se mariera.

Identifiers: Canadiana (print) 20190088583 | Canadiana (ebook) 20190088591 | ISBN 9781771664899 (softcover) | ISBN 9781771664905 (HTML) | ISBN 9781771664912 (PDF) | ISBN 9781771664929 (Kindle)

Classification: LCC PS8603.I357 E813 2019 | DDC C843/.6—dc23

Printed in Canada

To the men in my life

Yup, my name really is Aicha.

It's from that song, you know. No, you don't know. Nobody ever knows, but oh well. I know I really look like I should be called Emily or Camille, but I'm called Aicha. Aicha Saint-Pierre.

Saint-Pierre's my mother's last name, and Aicha…well, that's because my father's Algerian.

Well, okay, not my *father* father, but the guy my mother was with when she got pregnant with me.

He stayed for a while, I guess. Until he stopped hoping my hair and eyes would turn brown. And my skin.

He was nice.

He was hot too.

I have a photo of him in my purse. If you want to see it, I can show you sometime. Soon, like when they give me my purse back.

They *will* give me my purse back, right?

Because I have important stuff inside it. Will they go through it?

Whatever.

When my mother left to go who knows where—to work, according to her—the two of us stayed behind, him and me. I never went to school on those days, didn't even get dressed, and we watched movies all day and stuffed our faces with pizza and fries. The only thing he liked was those super old films like *Scarface*. I preferred cartoons, but he couldn't stand them, so I ended up getting used to his tastes.

And I ended up learning English too.

"You wanna fuck with me? Okay. You wanna play rough? Okay. Say hello to my little friend."

In the film, Tony Montana says that, then he pulls his gun out and blows everyone up.

One time with Hakim… Oh, I didn't tell you. His name was Hakim. To start off with, when I was little, I called him Dad, but everyone at school started laughing at me because he obviously couldn't be my real dad, so I stopped. I think he was hurt by that. He and my mother had a screaming match about it. He listed off all the insults he could think of, and then he started yelling in Arabic. But I wasn't really listening. After that he disappeared for a while, but then he came back. He always came back. Except for that time he didn't. That crazy woman had thrown all his stuff out the window, screeching like she was possessed. You should have seen her! She was a fucking mental case. She grabbed me really hard, and her nails dug into my arm and everything. "Go to your room and stay there," she yelled. She was seriously afraid I'd go with him, you know? And I would have if I'd known he was leaving for good.

…

I forget where I was.

Oh yeah.

So one time we were watching *Scarface* again, me and Hakim, pretty much the whole thing. We knew the words off by heart. Especially the bits where someone dies. There's like a bajillion people who die in that movie. It's basically my favourite movie now. Have you seen it?

Anyway. It's all good. The girl in it, the one who plays Elvira, apparently she looks like me. Her eyes and hair. And her breasts, for now, but I figure mine are going to be bigger than hers soon. But smaller than yours, I think. Yours are really big.

They're like that crazy bitch Élisanne Blais's, except yours are saggier and look softer. They look more like real ones.

Anyway.

I'd really like to show you my photo of Hakim. You can't see him too well because he's in profile, and anyway, my mother's half hiding him. But it's the only one I have of him. He had long hair, it was before I was born. It was taken in Kamouraska, or somewhere or other. Someplace beginning with K, I can't remember. I asked her about it again the other day, but she didn't answer me. Whenever I'm around, basically all she does is give me orders and then sigh. "Get out out of my way!" "Turn the TV off!" "Go and play somewhere else, I'm expecting someone!" "Feed the budgie!"

That fucking budgie. One day I'm going to barbecue that bird, I swear.

It spends all its time tweet-tweeting, or whatever sound budgies are supposed to make. The only way to make it shut up is to put a sheet over it.

One day I tried the same trick with my mother... You should have seen her beat the crap out of me afterwards! But it was *totally* worth it...

She was in the middle of doing her nails. I hate it when she does that. She thinks she's super important, even more than normal. She wanted me to bring her the phone, because she couldn't move because the polish was drying.

"Go and get it yourself," I said.

She started yelling at me. I picked up the bird's sheet—which wasn't even clean, it was all full of feathers and bird shit and crap—and then I threw it over her and said, "Shut your face!" Afterwards I got out of there fast, laughing my ass off.

I thought she might have forgotten, or gone out, when I got back from the library, but she hadn't. You should have seen the way she shook me! She was seriously losing it. It was violence against children. I could have made a complaint if I'd wanted to. But I don't really have any other family, so if I'd reported her they might have put me in a home with people I don't know, and I don't like people I don't know. But they don't like me either, so it doesn't bother me. And since I don't know anyone, well, I guess I don't like many people.

It's logical, right?

You seemed surprised when I said I went to the library. Do I look like I can't read or something?

No, no, I get what you mean. You weren't really expecting that when you saw me. It's not why I go there anyway. Well, yeah, I read sometimes, or I pretend to so people leave me alone. The armchairs they have there are super comfortable and they have Internet and everything. Not the whole Internet, but close. It's cool. Better than outside in winter.

Better than my house anyway.

You know those times when you feel like you have to be out of the house because your mother has a new guy over and she hasn't told him she has a rug rat, or she's ashamed, or she can't face seeing you, or she's trying to teach her fucking bird to talk and that makes you wanna smash your head into the wall until it starts bleeding… There aren't many other places you can go except the library.

Because I haven't got any friends.

Obviously, I have Melissa and Johannie, but they aren't always around. And they don't want me to hang out with them too much because it's not great for business. And because they don't want some guy to pick me up and make me do stupid shit because he thinks I'm a ho too. "Be careful, Aicha, there are some sick people out there," they tell me.

And they should know what they're talking about. You have to be a bit sick to want to sleep with a whore that's a guy dressed up as a girl, right?

They're cool and everything, but let's be honest, it's not like guys want to get sucked off by them because of their wonderful personalities.

No, I reckon you have to be kinda sick.

If you like guys, you like guys. I don't have a problem with that, I know tons of queers. If you like girls, you like girls, and that's fine too. But what's the point of picking up some woman on the street if she's not even a woman?

Apparently I'm too young to understand.

But I did ask the oldest guy I know, and he didn't get it either. It was Mr. Klop, the guy who owns the convenience store. I don't know how old he is exactly, but he's so old that he doesn't just have hair in his ears, it's actually *white* hair.

Klop's his real name. It's totally true. I'm not making it up, I swear. I take a lot of shit for being called Aicha Saint-Pierre, but just imagine if I was Aicha Klop! It's a Jewish name. So yeah, seems they're the chosen people and all, but if it means you have to be called Klop, they can keep it—their God and everything. And the old guy doesn't even believe in God anyway. Just think about that. He has to put up with being called Klop and it's all for nothing.

I'd be seriously mad.

But I'm mad all the time, apparently.

My mother says so, but she would, my teachers say it, even Melissa and Johannie say it, but all they do is insult people. What's that saying about clearing the crap away from your own door before sweeping your neighbour's porch?

Yeah, that. Whatever. You know what I mean.

…

Sometimes I'd like to rewind to when Hakim was still here.

Before I was mad all the time. Because it's true, I am mad all the time.

Everything was so cool back then, it seems like it can't really have happened, I just imagined the whole thing. Like someone else told me the story and I'm just pretending it was me. Or I saw it in a movie or something. With all the shit that went down afterwards, I told myself things couldn't ever have been that good.

You know what I mean?

Fine, you don't get it. I'm going to try to explain it to you just like a normal person.

It's like… Okay, imagine you're watching *Scarface* and you fall asleep right at the part when Tony gets married and everything's all happily ever after. And when you wake up he's being shot at from all sides. You wouldn't even think it was the same movie, even though it's the same actor and everything.

But okay, that's right, you haven't seen it. You wouldn't know. It was the exact same thing in my situation. Everything was going well. I didn't want anything, except to go back home and for Hakim to be there. For him to cut the crusts off my toast, or help me pull off my snowy boots, for us to snuggle in front of the TV and share a Twix, and for him to come and turn off my bedroom light and say, "Night night, kiddo."

That's happiness, right? Someone calling you kiddo with so much love in their voice that you whisper it to yourself over and over again like some kind of idiot until you fall asleep. I really did that, I swear.

And if that's not happiness, I don't know what is. If that's not happiness, I don't want anything to do with it.

Anyway, like I was saying, everything was just fine, and then there was nothing. No, not nothing, that's not true. Everything was shit. Just shit. Nothing but shit, everywhere, all the time. Everything was so shit that the less shitty days almost seemed good.

Who wouldn't be mad about being furious all the time, right?

Yes, I felt good when I was with "Sebastien."

It's weird, you calling him Sebastien. Nobody calls him that. His name's Baz. And you're making it sound like he's dead.

He isn't dead, is he?

You scared me there. But with my luck, I wouldn't have been surprised.

One time I told him he would totally get run over by a snowplow or get shot by a stray bullet someday. Obviously he asked why I said that. I wasn't going to say, "Because I love you," because I would've looked like a total loser. So I just shrugged my shoulders, and he laughed right in my face. But not meanly. He's never mean.

He's really not dead, right? You're sure?

…

He saved my life once. Yeah. That's how we met.

It's pretty boring here, isn't it? Can't you put some music on or something? I don't know how you can handle this silence. Doesn't it, like, distract you? For me, if there's not enough noise, it's like having a fridge humming in my head, until all the things I'm thinking about just rattle around in there.

That's not super fun.

But anyway, here I am talking to you, so it's fine; it's stopping me from thinking about stuff.

What do you want me to tell you? About the time he saved my life? Or everything? Should I tell you everything?

I'd be happy to.

But I'm warning you, I don't know the exact dates or anything. I suck at remembering dates and that kind of stuff. One time Baz tried to teach me guitar and I sucked pretty bad. You're going to say that's got nothing to do with it, but dates are kind of like knowing which finger goes on which fret, and which string to press and all that. I preferred listening to him play. Or maybe I should say watching him play.

Or resting my head on his shoulder while he played, and singing along, but just quietly, some song that isn't supposed to be played or sung quietly. Like, if you whisper the lyrics to a heavy metal song, it sounds seriously poetic.

Anyway.

It makes me feel all tingly in the pit of my stomach whenever I hear an amp buzzing. It's like a hot dead space. A hole… I dunno. And the first chord he always strums before he really starts playing. It's always the same one. The way he strums the chords, quietly but not too quietly. I'm not, like, trying to impress you with everything I know about music. But it's important if you want to understand why I love him.

Well, that's why, because of how he strums chords, and a ton of other stupid tiny little things like the little repaired chip in his tooth that's a completely different colour than the rest. I have a list, I can show it to you if you like. It's in my purse too. You'll see, there's all these sheets of paper, all these different-coloured pens, because I studied him for a long time. I didn't put little hearts on the i's or any of that kind of stupid shit. I'm not a total loser. Girls in school do that. And they write each other letters about their crushes and lose their shit when the guy walks past. I don't do that. I don't have anyone to write letters to. But I don't care, it's stupid anyway. And I don't lose my shit when I bump into Baz.

Anyway, we never bumped into each other. Never never never.

We always *met up*.

If you bump into someone, it's, like, not deliberate. But we didn't do that. We always met up on purpose. Mr. Klop thinks it's fate. Hakim always used to say that God meddles in our business to arrange things his way. "Insh'Allah, God willing," he said. I don't really believe that, or else God's just a piece of shit. But fine…fate, chance, God, or some alien kid with tons of cash who plays with us like we're just an ant farm, whatever, Baz and me never just bumped into each other.

You should write that down, it's important.

Have you written it down?

…

If you want, I can lend you my list of reasons why I love him. Or I could mail it to you, maybe. Then you won't have to write it out again if you need it. I don't care, it's not like it's personal or anything. One time I shouted out to the whole city that I loved him. Well, okay, to the whole neighbourhood, but when it's dark our neighbourhood is kind of like the city.

I told him I never looked at the sky, and he thought that was sad. But looking at the sky seemed stupid to me. Like staring at the TV screen when it's turned off. Sometimes a plane goes by, but then you can just say, "Look, there's a plane," and you don't give a shit because it's never you in the plane.

Well, it's never me.

What I mean is, it's boring looking at the sky. Everybody goes on about the stars and everything. In movies you always see it when the guy and the chick are in love. But I don't think anybody in Montreal can be in love, because I've never seen people gazing at the fucking stars. That's why I don't look at the sky. It's depressing that nobody in this city is in love. So that's more or less what I said to Baz. Maybe I explained it better, but you know.

So he took me up on the roof of his building so we could look at the sky, him and me. I teased him a little, because it was cheesy as shit, but it was cool. More than cool, actually.

…

Okay, well, at the beginning it was shitty.

He was looking at the sky and he wasn't doing anything. Or saying anything. At one point, a plane went by, and he didn't even say, "Look, there's a plane." I didn't dare point it out to him. I thought maybe it was like in church when you have to be silent, or something.

I started to get irritated. I pretended to be cold so I'd have something to do, I rubbed my neck to give me an excuse to stop looking up in the air, I tried to look at a different, less boring part of the sky, but I don't think there are any. Then I looked around, and you know what? I'd never seen Montreal at night from so high up.

I cried a little bit.

I mean, not *cried* cried. Just a little bit. Like from emotion.

I went up to him, he was still looking up at the sky, and I pointed out all the lights of the street lamps, the cars, the buildings, and I said, "That's where the stars are."

And then we kissed. For the first time. It was like in the movies. Except for the whores downstairs bawling out their gay neighbour who's always calling for his cat at night. And there was a smell of piss. And the music wasn't like from some romantic movie, it was just an old drunk crazy lady singing "My Heart Will Go On" in a karaoke bar.

Our kiss lasted a few seconds and then he put his arm around my shoulders. And that whole time, and for hours afterwards, I felt like everything I could see belonged to me.

I wanted to lean out into the void and yell, "I am the queen of the world!" but for one thing it was fucking high up, and for another I didn't even like *Titanic*. Or not that part anyway, even if it is a part with a girl in it. So I shouted, "I love you!"

Some guy told me to shut the fuck up, so I told him to go fuck himself.

...

Okay, that part's not true. I didn't shout that.

But it would have been fun. I wanted to shout it. If we'd really made out, I think I would have done it.

Except we didn't.

Hey, I didn't make everything up, you know. That story about the roof and everything is true. It's all true except we didn't make out. But the whores yelling and the smell of piss and the karaoke woman, that's all true.

And his arm around my shoulders.

And Montreal really did belong to me that whole time.

Well, you know what I mean.
Do you know what I mean?

…

Wait, I haven't finished telling you. If you get me confused I'll leave bits out. I'm supposed to tell you how Baz and I met.

It's a cool story. Nearly as cool as the roof story. Without the making out.

It was a Thursday. I remember that because earlier in the day I'd borrowed two bucks from Jo. I told her I'd pay her back, and she said, "Don't worry, it's Thursday, it's payday." And then she seemed to find it super funny, Mel too. I didn't get it though.

Anyway, all that's just to say it was a Thursday and that's why I remember.

It wasn't true that I was going to pay back the two dollars. I've discovered that two dollars is the amount you can borrow and say you're going to pay it back but never actually pay it back. Nobody ever makes a fuss about two bucks.

You just have to make sure not to ask the same person twice, or else ask them when they're in a really good mood. This trick works the same way with my mother, I swear. She feels so guilty about being a bitch that sometimes I even get five. Of course, she always asks what I'm going to do with it. And I don't want to tell her.

I'm not doing anything with it, that's the problem. It's just fun to see who will lend you money and how much. It's like I'm doing a study or something. Anyway, at two bucks a pop I won't be going on an African safari any time soon.

I don't want to go to Africa anyway.

So it was a Thursday. But that's not important, I was just giving you a bit of context. Like an introduction.

I don't really like hanging around in the street with nothing to do. In winter it's cold and there's tons of people I don't know, and in summer it's too hot and there are even more people I don't know. And they're sweating too. So it stinks. I hate that.

So anyway, there I was outside, I guess I must have been feeling adventurous or something.

Okay, for real, I just wanted to sit down on the bouncy duck at the park. I don't often feel like thinking, but when it comes on, it goes better on the back of a duck. I think it's the rocking motion maybe. I guess it helps me think better. Tons of ideas come to me. Sometimes it helps me chill out. Otherwise I wouldn't go there; it's always a mess afterwards. You come back with your shoes full of sand and you find it everywhere for like the next two weeks, even in your ass crack.

Okay, so maybe not two weeks, but it feels like two weeks.

Anyway, shoes full of sand is still better than stepping on a syringe. At least, that's what people say. Because I've never personally stepped on a syringe. I bet you haven't either.

It's the kind of story that frightens everyone but never actually happens to anyone. An urban legend, they call it. There's syringes around, of course, but nobody's ever got one stuck in their foot. Because I can't see who'd be stupid enough to prance around with bare feet in a sandbox. With all the dog shit and condoms and everything. And the syringes, obviously.

See, it makes no sense.

So I was sitting on my duck and thinking about stuff. Actually, I was rocking and trying to see if my brain would touch the inside of my skull when I moved my head. I looked like a jerk, now that I think about it.

Some guy came and sat on the horse next to me. The kind of guy who pisses in the street and without even hiding his dick and who smells like shitty wine and crack.

"You got any money?" he asked me.

I said no. I had the two bucks I'd got from Jo but I didn't want to give him that. He got up and made like he was going, then came back and said, "You sure?"

I replied, "Yup, I'm sure, fuck off, you stinky old man," or something along those lines, and carried on rocking. He started yelling at me. I wanted to get up, but I told myself he couldn't do anything to me if I stayed sitting on my duck. You know you can't rape a girl who's sitting down, it's got to find a way in somewhere. He could have pulled me off the duck, or beaten me to death, or forced me to suck him off, or stolen my two bucks, or some combination of all the above.

So I was pretty much in the shit.

I couldn't see anyone else around apart from this guy, and I couldn't hear anything except him yelling. Nobody had ever hit me before, I wondered if it hurt. I was pretty sure it would hurt.

Maybe someone would have taken me to the hospital where my mother works. I might be so smashed up that I'd only be able to say, "Jean Taloooon…Hooo…ooospitaaaaal," with like a sigh, like they do in movies. Because that's where my mother works. They wouldn't have taken me there anyway because Notre Dame is right nearby, but it would have been pretty spectacular. And then once I'd turned up, my mother would have started crying so hard because I was gonna die and everything, and before I croaked I would have just said, "Mom, I–I…"

And then I would've died.

And she'd never have known what I was going to say.

So you can imagine I was a bit disappointed when I heard someone yelling, "Hey!" Okay, so I wasn't really disappointed, because I didn't like the part where I had to get my head kicked in, but let's say I do die one day, without intending to, I'm gonna pull that shit with my mother.

Anyway, basically, the "Hey!" was Baz.

All my life I'm going to remember the feeling I had when I saw him. For real. When I'm dying I'll still remember it. I'm gonna do that thing with my mother, yeah, for sure, but after, I'm gonna remember the first time I saw Baz. I don't know how to explain the feeling to you. It was like I'd just gotten bitten by a vampire who'd sucked out all my blood and replaced it with Coke. Like that time I was going through my mother's stuff and a cardboard box full of winter clothes smashed me in the head. BANG!

You know what they say about love at first sight?

That.

I nearly smashed my face on my duck.

I went a bit deaf, and my vision was kind of blurry, so I don't know exactly what happened, but the bad guy went away and I just nodded my head when Baz—although I didn't know he was called Baz then—asked me if I was okay.

He walked off, and I got down off my duck and followed him. Like a cat.

Did you know cats do that sometimes? They follow you but you don't know why. You stop, turn around, look at them, and they stop and look at you. You carry on, they carry on, you stop, they stop…

That's what I did. I followed him all the way to his house without trying to hide, but at a reasonable distance. Not on purpose. Not like some crazy stalker.

Okay, maybe a bit.

But I needed to stay close. Do you realize if I hadn't followed him I might never have seen him again! I would've preferred to get chopped up into pieces, chopped into pieces and eaten by that guy in the park. Or something even worse, you know what I mean.

He went back to his place. I was afraid it wasn't his place, that it was just a friend's house or something, and that he'd never come back to this area again.

I stood across the road for a while, watching the windows and wondering which one he was behind.

He ended up looking out of the middle one and gave me a wave.

I didn't respond, and then I ran off.

Anyway, I think cats are stupid.

Could I get another glass of water?

Or a juice?

I think it would be nicer to have juice, because it seems to me we're gonna be here for a while.

It's not like I want to tell my life story, but I don't really have much choice if I want to get Baz out of trouble, right? You do believe me when I say he didn't do anything, right?

…

It's funny the way you open your eyes really wide. At the beginning I thought it was because I was saying something stupid, but you do it all the time, even when I'm not saying stupid things. Do you have dry eyes?

When my mother has dry eyes she puts drops in them. Why don't you try drops? I can wait two minutes while you go to the washroom and do it, if you want. Don't do it in front of me, it makes me wanna throw up, people poking around in their eyes, it's disgusting. And then on your way back you could see if there's any juice.

Or maybe I could go look myself?

Alright, I'll stay here. But stop doing that thing with your eyes. I'm not kidding, it totally freaks me out.

I have this dream quite a lot. It's a nightmare really. I have eyeballs on my tongue and I can't talk. My mouth is full of them and I can't get them out. I try to shout but it doesn't work, I can't close my mouth, so I try and swallow them but there's too many, I chew them but it's super disgusting, it's squishy and then it squirts, it makes me barf and I end up suffocating in my vomit full of eyes.

That's really gross, isn't it?

One time I googled to see if it meant anything, but I didn't find anything. What do you think it means?

I don't really care anyway. It's only a dream.

So after…yeah…

I went back to stand outside his building. Like once or twice. Okay, maybe more.

I needed to see him again. To say thanks.

Or just to see him again.

But after a while I got fed up. When you've been squatting outside someone's place for two weeks, morning, noon, afternoon, and night, you start to lose hope, don't you?

Anyway…

I decided to drop the whole thing and went back to think on my duck. I was lovesick.

I'd pinched my mother's pack of smokes and I'd tried to trick Mr. Klop into selling me beer, because drinking is something people do when they're lovesick. The old douchebag refused so I bought some Canada Dry. At least he put the can in a paper bag for me.

Having a broken heart was already a pretty terrible feeling, but with the taste of the cigarettes too it was seriously revolting.

I was going to chuck the cigarette away but I thought I looked cute with it. I thought smoking made me look more like Elvira (you know, Tony Montana's girlfriend, I told you about her earlier). I was looking at my reflection in a car window so I didn't see him coming.

When I'm doing something, I have no idea of anything that's going on around me. It's like this flaw I have. I'm not like some bird or a fly, you know, with eyes all around its head. Or spiders, they have as many eyes as they have legs. Do spiders have the same number of eyes as legs?

Whatever.

He came and sat on the horse next to the duck and said hello. I jumped and looked at him without replying. He said he was sorry, he didn't mean to scare me.

"You didn't scare me," I said.

"What's your name?"

"Aicha."

"How old are you?"

"Eighteen."

Normally I'm pretty good at holding back on the lies. I exaggerate sometimes, but my arrangement of the truth is usually pretty reasonable. But I panicked then and said eighteen. I might as well have said, "Fifty-nine, but I have a congenital illness." It would have been about as believable. He looked amazed. I shrugged and said, "Fine, I'm fifteen."

That answer seemed to suit him. Which was lucky, since I had better things to do than argue about my age all night.

"Can I have a cigarette?" he asked.

"Here, take the whole pack, I've decided to quit."

He laughed.

I wanted to ask him his name and everything, but my voice was garbage. I didn't want it to come out all weird. You know when you want to say something but it won't come out? When you want to, like, tell someone you love them, but you are physically incapable of doing it because the words are too big for your mouth, or because you feel like it's going to set off an avalanche of emotions and bury you?

No? Maybe it's just me then.

Anyway, I was totally tongue-tied and couldn't even ask him what his name was. Luckily he read my mind. Otherwise…

That time, we just talked for a little while. Actually he asked questions and I answered. But my heart was beating so fast I thought it was gonna explode, so I have no idea what I was saying. After that I tried to contain the damage: I just nodded my head.

At one point, it got too emotional and I don't like emotions, so I said I had to go. But I asked him if he'd be there the next day.

I wanted to ask him the same question about the next day and the next day, until the end of time, but I didn't do that either. If I always did what I wanted, people would think I was mentally ill.

When I got back to the house, I was so happy that I sat next to my nutbar mother on the couch. She seemed really pleased and asked how I was doing. I said I was fine.

But then she smelled smoke on me and started yelling.

I shut myself in my room, and because it's horrible to be shouted at when you've been so happy, I cried.

Can you see how annoying she is? She always comes along and ruins everything. She was all set to ruin everything with Baz just like she did with Hakim.

"You didn't send her to school today either?" "What have

you been doing all day?" "Get dressed, Aicha, you can't parade around in your underwear all day, you're too old for that."

I liked wandering around the house in my underwear because his skin touched my skin when we hugged on the couch. Sometimes his fingers tickled me. Fun tickling.

…

You do know I'm talking about Hakim, right?

I didn't wander around in my underwear in front of Baz, are you crazy? Jo says you have to cultivate a bit of mystery. Which is a bit "Do what I say, not what I do," because when it comes to mystery she can hardly talk, with her skirt that you can't even tell if it's a skirt or a belt and her lace camisole showing off her empty bra.

Yeah, cultivate a bit of mystery. I'm always doing that, no need to tell me to do it. I play hard to get. That's a tip from Melissa. It means you pretend you don't give a shit even when you do.

I have a ton of examples.

At the beginning of our relationship, I spent whole days waiting for him to show up. But I pretended that's not what I was doing.

It was pretty hard, because there's seriously nothing to do on the street or in the park with the ducks when you aren't a kid anymore. I mean, I could have lined up rocks or done sociological experiments with ants, but I didn't exactly want Baz thinking I was only twelve or something.

Because I was supposed to be fifteen.

Once I met him in the street with his guitar on his back. I asked him where he was going, but just like I was trying to make conversation, not like my life depended on his answer or anything.

"I'm going to get the blah blah blah of my guitar's blah blah blah fixed," he said.

"Right," I said, making out like I knew what he was talking about.

"What are you doing?"

"Oh, you know, the usual. I can't go home because my mother has some guy over and they're screwing in the living room."

"Uh…okay."

He seemed pretty uncomfortable. I dialled it up a notch. "Right now I'm waiting for Melissa and Johannie, and I'll probably hang with them for a bit while they're waiting for customers."

"Who're Melissa and Johannie?"

"My whore friends."

"Uh…right, well…"

"I've never been in a music store."

He asked me if I wanted to go with him. I said I didn't know (playing hard to get) but in the end I said yes.

We walked to the Berri-UQAM metro station and got on a train. It was like our first date or something.

He left his guitar at the repair desk and then it was all super long and boring. The bearded guy in the store showed him tons of new stuff, got him to try out loads of instruments. I didn't dare touch anything because I was afraid of making a noise or breaking some pretty little $8,000 widget.

When we left, he asked me if I was hungry.

He was hungry.

"Have you ever been to the Marché Jean Talon? They have the best merguez sandwiches in town."

My throat hurt.

Hakim always said they didn't know how to make merguez sandwiches in Quebec, or if you could get a good one you had to sell a kidney to pay for it. That was one of the things that used to make him mad.

"You don't know what you're talking about if you've never

been to Algeria. People in Quebec don't know anything," I replied, shrugging my shoulders.

He gave me a funny look. With a little smile that said, *It's kinda funny that you take me for an idiot.*

"So have you ever been to Algeria, Aicha?"

"No."

"And have you ever had a merguez sandwich?"

"No."

"So you're a real Québécoise. You don't know what you're talking about." And he laughed.

I sulked a bit because it annoys me when people laugh at me.

If I'd known how to get home I would've left right then.

He carried on talking but I pretended not to listen. He was telling me about the history of the area. I had a ton of nasty comebacks like *If it's really the best neighbourhood in the world, why did you move away? Come back!* But you don't tease people when you're sulking.

We finally arrived at his merguez place and he ordered two sandwiches. He said, "Do you want something to drink with it? A Coke?"

The guy behind the counter said he didn't have Coke, only Selecto.

My throat hurt again. I said, "The Selecto here doesn't taste anything like the stuff in Algeria."

He gave me a funny look, both of them did. If I wasn't still seriously mad at him, I would've told him to go fuck himself.

We sat down on concrete slabs and ate our sandwiches. I swear, I didn't want to like it. I did everything I could to not like it.

"Well, it wasn't too bad, I guess," Baz said, when I'd eaten my whole sandwich.

"Hmmm."

"What's with all the Algeria stuff? Do you wanna tell me?"

"Hmmm."

"You want another one?"

"Mmm-hmm."

I waited for him on the concrete slab while he went to get us both another sandwich.

I was super frustrated, but I still thought he was hot. I thought that since I'd never go to Algeria, it was enough to just enjoy the Quebec merguez-sandwich talent. Because in the end, that day, sitting with my ass on a slab of concrete, it was the best sandwich I've ever eaten in my life.

I didn't tell him about all the Algeria stuff that time. You don't cultivate mystery by telling someone your whole life story the first chance you get.

After we'd met up a few times he invited me over to his place. It was actually a few weeks after the music store. I asked him if his guitar was fixed and he said yes.

"Are you any good?" I asked.

He shrugged his shoulders and my stomach rumbled. I don't know why, I wasn't even hungry. At lunch I'd eaten some leftover shepherd's pie my mother had made for me the night before, because I like it better when it's reheated.

Don't tell her that I said this, but my mother's shepherd's pie is totally kick-ass. It's annoyed me for years that something she makes could be so good. It's like Hitler, you know. Maybe his chocolate cake was kick-ass too, even if it wasn't very well known. Nobody would want to eat the best chocolate cake in the world if Hitler had made it, would they?

Well, it's the same thing with my mother's cooking.

He asked me if I was hungry.

"No."

"You can tell me if you are. Are you hungry?"

"Well, not really. I ate some toast and peanut butter last

night. My mother forgot to buy bread, so that's what I was going to get."

I opened my hand to show him the two bucks I'd just borrowed from the neighbour. "I told her that my mother forgot to get milk and I didn't have enough money in my piggy bank, and asked her if she'd loan me a dollar. Said I'd pay her back next month when I get my pocket money. She gave me a toonie and told me to keep it."

I don't know why some people beat up seniors to take their money when all you need to do is make them feel sorry for you.

Anyway.

He asked me when my mother was coming back and I shrugged. "Dunno."

He swore a bit and then asked me to have dinner at his place.

So pity doesn't just work with old people.

That evening he asked me tons of questions again. At least until he realized that I was barely half answering because the questions were annoying me. Lying is exhausting, but seeing people's faces change when you tell the truth is depressing.

It got late but I didn't want to leave. I asked him to play me a song. Then another. And then another one.

I could have listened to him all night.

Except things never go the way I want them to. He got a text and then he took me back home.

"I'll wait down here. When you're upstairs, wave at me through the window."

"Why?"

"Because."

I went up and waved, and then he left, not toward his place.

I wanted to follow him, obviously, but I just watched him until he'd gone around the corner. And for a while afterwards, hoping that he'd come back.

With all that crap, I didn't hear my mother come home.

"Aicha, why are you still up? What are you staring at? Why didn't you eat the pasta bake for dinner? Have you done your homework?"

Like I said before, lying is exhausting, and seeing people's faces change when you tell the truth is depressing.

So I just said, "Your pasta bake is gross," and went to bed.

I hoped she'd make it again though.

Because Baz is perfect except for one thing: he's a horrible cook.

Once I showed up at his place and he was cutting meat with some bougie knife that I wasn't allowed to touch, maybe because it was too precious, but probably because it was too sharp.

"What are you doing?" I asked.

"Steak tartare. Have you ever had it?"

"No. But it looks like when my mother makes meatballs."

"I thought your mother didn't cook."

I shrugged.

See what I mean about lying being exhausting? Well, there's a good example. I'd forgotten I'd told him my mother didn't cook. When you feel comfortable with someone, sometimes you lower your guard and forget your lies.

Right then I decided to never tell him another lie.

Or at least try.

Well, fine. Anyway, where was I?

Oh yeah, so did you know you eat steak tartare raw? You don't, like, cook it or anything. It's like sushi, but meat. And do you know all the diseases you can get from eating raw meat?

You could die.

And not just die. Die after suffering like an earthworm that's been chopped in half. Worse maybe, because I don't even know if earthworms suffer. Anyway, you know what I mean.

That's also why I decided not to lie to him anymore. I didn't want to have to eat that crap and maybe die from it, just because I was pretending to be starving to make him feel sorry for me. Anyway, our relationship had moved on from that.

While he was cutting up potatoes for his fries (I didn't even know you could make fries yourself but I didn't say anything so I wouldn't look stupid) he told me he wanted to be a chef.

I didn't even know what a chef was but according to him it's a cook, only hotter. He laughed and said I didn't look very convinced.

"I like it when you play the guitar more than when you cook."

"Then my challenge is to make you like both equally!"

He tried to stuff a chunk of his raw meat into my mouth and I whacked my face falling off the stool trying to get away from him.

When I look back at it, it makes me think of those movies where the lovers spray each other with whipped cream and end up fucking in it. Except at the time I was thinking about the raw meat killing me.

...

Yeah, no, you're right, it's not really the same thing.

I also told him what I wanted to do. Like, when I grow up.

"I don't really know what I want to be. I used to want to be a whore, but that doesn't seem that fun after all. Mel and Jo are always complaining about clients who disrespect them and everything.

"Actually I do want to be a whore, but one who just has one client. A respectful client. One who would ask how my day was and run me a bath. I'd cook for him and look after the house, or maybe we'd have a cleaner. I'd be in love with him, he'd be in love with me, and he'd let me do whatever I wanted, like go to Africa on vacation, or watch old films all day long, or whatever. We'd have a fabulous life and I'd never have to worry about anything again. Financially speaking or any other way.

"We'd have a contract that said I was his only whore and he was my only client, and he had to look after me and vice versa. It would be the law.

"But worst case, if that's too complicated, we get married."

Baz took a sip of his drink and said, as if to himself, something like, "Gloria Steinem would be proud."

I don't know who she is and I don't give a shit if she'd be proud. I shrugged.

It was really nice, all those nights I spent listening to him play the guitar or watching him try his hand at cooking inedible food, but after a while I wanted more.

After a while, I wanted a whole night.

I laid the groundwork by provoking a screaming match with my mother. I could have lied to Baz but I was still seriously into my resolution not to lie to him anymore.

I threw a glass at the TV screen while *Grey's Anatomy* was on. The screen shattered into ten thousand pieces.

I don't know if it was the fact that I'd wrecked the flat screen or because I'd made her miss the end of her favourite show… I can't see the point of watching that stupid show if you actually work in a hospital. Do you watch TV shows about social workers? Is that even a thing?

Anyway.

I'm sure she does it because she wanted to be a nurse, but instead she got pregnant with me and got stuck wiping old people's asses. That's why she makes my life impossible. Because I wrecked hers.

Basically, my plan succeeded, I broke the TV and she yelled. She was even going on about how I must be possessed. I tried to get her to hit me hard enough to leave a mark, but she doesn't have the balls to do that. She cries instead.

She's always crying.

If I'd had the energy I would've felt sorry for her.

…

She left for work and ten minutes later I showed up at Baz's place, crying. I told him my mother had blown a fuse and smashed the TV.

Yeah, you're doing that thing with your eyes again. Are your eyes dry or do you think it was bad to say that? But it's not really a lie. I mean, it did really happen.

Anyway, that's what I did. "Can I sleep here?" I asked.

"Do you have school tomorrow?"

"No."

"No?"

"Okay, I do, but it's not important. We're just doing flower arranging or some shit."

"You kill me, Aicha."

"In the good meaning?"

He just… I don't know what you call it when you do that. Like a sort of half-amused, half-resigned sigh.

To start off with, he wanted to sleep on the couch, but I told him I was very small and wouldn't take up much space in his bed. He said that wasn't the problem. I asked what the problem was but he didn't answer me.

Do you know what the problem was? He was afraid of getting a hard-on. Guys get embarrassed if they get a hard-on around a girl they're not dating. I said, "Don't worry, it's no big deal, you don't need to be embarrassed if you get hard, I like it."

So he slept on the couch.

I thought and thought all night but I couldn't figure out where I'd messed up.

He lent me his T-shirt to sleep in.

With his shirt, in his sheets, in his smell, I felt like he was with me, like he was touching me. Softly, just brushing my skin. I murmured his name.

He got into bed with me. He kissed my neck and lifted up my shirt to lick my breasts. Even though they're still small, it was pretty great. He slipped his fingers inside my panties. My breathing was getting heavy, but I didn't know if that was right, if I was supposed to make noise, so I tried to hold back. I wanted to touch him too but I didn't dare. So he took my hand and put it on his…thing. I didn't know what to do with it and I was embarrassed. He said it was no big deal, we'd take it slow. He carried on stroking me. When he lingered in a certain place it was like electricity surging through me and I had to stop myself from yelling. It was like nothing I'd ever experienced. Like play tickling but times a thousand. The more he played with me, the wetter I got. So wet that it was trickling between my butt cheeks. I didn't know if it was supposed to do that and I was afraid it might stain his sheets but he didn't seem bothered. He whispered in my ear that I should let myself relax, and he pushed his whole finger in. It felt so good I cried out.

It was sick how good it felt.

Has anyone ever done that to you?

Okay, you don't have to answer that.

He kept saying, "Just relax, just relax, just relax." He pushed two fingers in. Two seems like a lot but it was even better. I wanted him to put them all in but I didn't dare ask. My belly was begging him to put them all in.

I must have sighed a bit too loudly, or breathed in too deeply, I'm not sure what happened.

He shouted from the living room, "Aicha, are you okay?"

I said breathlessly, "Yes, I'm fine, good night," and fell asleep with my fingers still inside me.

Did anything ever happen with Baz outside my imagination?

What, you think I'm crazy?

Like I imagined the whole thing.

You're getting on my nerves with all your questions. I'm telling you all these super personal things and you sit there accusing me of lying.

And we've been doing this for like a thousand years and you haven't even given me any juice or anything.

I'm thirsty, I'm thirsty, I'm thirsty, I'm thirsty, I'm thirsty, I'm thirsty, I'm thirsty, I'm thirsty.

...

Thanks. It was about time, but thanks.

...

Why do they make orange juice with pulp? Who even likes pulp, seriously? It's like selling lumpy mashed potato or pancake batter. Pancake batter sounds kind of silly if you say it fast. Try it.

...

You're so boring. Can't we joke around? Do you have any friends? A boyfriend? A girlfriend? You can tell me if you prefer girls, you can tell me, I won't tell anyone. Anyway, I don't see who I would tell, seeing as we don't have any mutual friends.

So are you a lesbian or not? Go on! I've been telling you a

whole bunch of super personal stuff for ages, you can tell me. Yes or no?

It's no big deal, I don't care, you can screw whoever you want.

"You can screw whoever you want!"

Baz said that to me once. Or "Do what you want," I can't really remember. But anyway, he meant, "You can screw whoever you want." Because he was jealous, I know it.

I'll tell you what happened.

I'd already slept over at his place a couple of times, and it was cool and everything but it wasn't really going anywhere.

…

And yes, my mother knew I was staying at his place. Well, she knew I wasn't sleeping at home. She'd never have let me go there, that killjoy. I told her I was sleeping at Jo's. She doesn't know Jo's a whore, she thinks she's a girl my age, obviously. I was so sick of her telling me I needed to make friends that I told her I had some, that their names were Melissa and Johannie, just so she'd shut up. I would've liked to bring them home for dinner one night just to see her face.

"Doll yourself up, Mel." "Wear those shorts with the hole in the ass, Jo," I could have said. Then we could have eaten sausages and they could have spent the whole meal explaining how to give good head and how much lube you need so it doesn't hurt when someone takes you up the ass and it's still fun.

They told me that one day, just in case. "Education starts young," Melissa said. "She's going to do it sometime, and most likely it's not going to be with a guy who knows how to do it properly, so if you don't want her to end up bleeding out of her ass I'd rather tell her now."

Ending up bleeding out of my ass didn't appeal, so I soaked up all the information. I asked a ton of questions even if the whole thing made me feel a bit sick, but in reality I wanted to know what the first time was like the front way. Because back then I hadn't done it yet, so I was curious.

But yeah, Mel and Jo, since they weren't real girls, couldn't really tell me much. They have tons of advice to give about all kinds of stuff, but "when it comes to that vagina stuff, you're on your own, honey."

I would've liked my first time to be with Baz. It would have been romantic. Sometimes romantic is cool. But Centre-Sud isn't exactly Hollywood. When the music starts playing whenever something good happens, it's more likely to be the gay neighbour singing his heart out to some Celine Dion song, not Steven Tyler.

He's the lead singer of Aerosmith.

Yup, I knew you were going to make that face.

You know, in that movie, the one with the end of the world when a big meteorite's heading to earth and everything, and they send the boyfriend of that elf from *Lord of the Rings* and her father who was also in *Lethal Weapon* or something.

No, wait, it wasn't *Lethal Weapon*, I'm getting mixed up. Whatever.

Why is it never the end of the world in Centre-Sud, hey? I feel like we deserve a good apocalypse. Or at least I deserve one. Not that I want to die, but it would be a good excuse for screwing.

I've thought about that a lot.

Like on TV, you'd have Peter Mansbridge announcing that there was a tsunami on the way or a supervolcano about to blow its top. Supervolcanoes freak me right out. Anyway. So he's announcing that and everyone starts screaming and crying and running in the streets, and I just go over to Baz's place and we kiss, and then we fuck until the world blows up, and he pretends to make animal crackers drink sweat from my navel, and we say we love each other and all that shit.

And at some point we see the sky getting darker, and everything sounds muffled, like when you block your ears. Everything starts shaking, and then there's this big, big light, sparks, flashes, and everything. I press myself against him and then, bang! We can die.

Because obviously we would die, right. When the apocalypse comes to Montreal we'll die. Nobody's gonna show up to save us at the last minute, the government, the police, or whoever. Like even if they could save people from the disaster, they'd choose queers, whores, junkies, and welfare bums.

No, no, no. When the apocalypse comes we'll be the first to get blown up, obviously.

I talked to Baz about it once. I asked him if he was ever afraid of the world ending.

He laughed and then told me I thought too much. He stopped noodling on his guitar and then asked me if it really bothered me. I just shrugged. I wasn't going to admit it to him.

He came over and gave me a hug, then tried to reassure me. He wouldn't have done that if he'd seen the show I watched about supervolcanoes. He would've said, "Yeah, you're right, we could all die any second."

Weirdly, that would have reassured me.

I told him that if the end of the world did come, I'd like to be with him.

You know what he did?

He laughed and patted me on the head, like you pat a dog. Like, pat pat pat, snicker, and then he went off and sat down with his guitar.

I swear, for real that nearly was the end of the world. I almost exploded. With all the pain I had inside I would've blown up a lot of shit. I would've taken out not just Centre-Sud but also the whole of Montreal. The city would be flattened right out as far as Outremont.

They wouldn't have seen that one coming.

Mansbridge wouldn't have called that one!

I wanted to him tell him he was a bastard, but I would've cried, and I don't do crying.

I got the fuck out of there without saying anything, or maybe just, like, "I'm not your dog." Yeah, I think that's what I said, and then I walked out.

I bumped into Mel and Jo, I didn't say hi to them because I couldn't think of any words except *fucking cunt fucking cunt fucking cunt*. I walked until my tongue hurt.

It was a long way. I had to take two buses and a subway to get back home.

Why is it that sometimes you give everything, absolutely everything, to someone so that there's nothing left for you, not even yourself, and he doesn't want it? He throws it all right back in your fucking face without even bothering to explain why or anything. Just gives you a pat on the head before going back to playing his crappy songs on his shitty fucking guitar.

Why would you make someone pasta with ham that you'd cut up into tiny pieces, so small that you could taste the parmesan and everything, and tell them you love them, and then it's not even true?

Why would you hug someone, watch movies with her, make her happier than she'll ever be again, say, "Night night, kiddo," or "I'm right here, Aicha," and then when she tells you she'll die if you leave, you leave anyway?

…

I'm not crying.

…

I feel like throwing up.

It's the fucking pulp in your juice.

I can't tell you about the first time I made love because I've never made love.

I'd tell you if I'd done it, but it's never happened.

The brother of that guy from school doesn't count. That was just to piss Baz off. And it did piss him off, so it worked. You know that feeling when you win but there's a taste in your mouth like you lost? That.

It was an afternoon, I don't really know when but it was summer or pretty close to it. We were over at his place, we'd watched a movie, and then he was getting ready to go out someplace where I couldn't go, somewhere with his friends.

He lifted up his arm for some reason or other and I saw the bottom of his stomach, the side of it, just there. It was so hot that my throat and my stomach clenched.

It took my mind off things.

"I just said you're hot."

"Thanks. You're pretty cute yourself."

"We'd be good together."

"Yeah, maybe, if you were older…"

It wasn't long after the head-patting incident. I was expecting that kind of answer from him. It didn't take me by surprise like it had the first time.

"If I was older, I wouldn't be as beautiful," I said.

"Aicha…"

"I'd have wrinkles, my skin would be saggy, and I'd have a flat ass and droopy breasts. They're definitely not droopy now."

They really weren't droopy. But you know something, I'm telling you this whole story and I forgot to say I was still a little girl at the time. I still wore sweatpants, the kind of thing you can't even tell whether it's pyjamas, real clothes, or just some towels sewn together. I was still a caterpillar in my cocoon, or whatever Melissa calls it. It's, like, a metaphor.

But anyway, that time he got annoyed. He wasn't mean about it, because he's never mean, but he told me to cut it out.

"Aicha, you have to stop all this. I like you a lot, we hang out together, and I think you're cute for a little girl. But you need to get it out of your head that we could ever be anything other than friends. It creeps me out just thinking about it. It's sick, Aicha. I'm more than twice your age. I'd get into shit for it, it would fuck with your head, and mine too. Have you ever thought of that? Fuck! You spend so much time thinking about pointless crap, spend two minutes thinking about *that*! Find yourself some friends who aren't whores or drunks and then fall in love with some guy your own age, do stuff kids your age do. And fuck, take your time. Aicha, I wish I could fix some of the shitty things that have happened to you in your life. I don't want to add more. Do you get where I'm coming from?"

No.

In my head I'm a thousand years old. I don't know how many times older than him that makes me.

I don't see why it's such a big deal.

Anyway. That night I decided to be the age I was in my head. I screwed someone.

It's not hard to screw when you need to or when you feel

like it. You can even get money for it.

I borrowed the clothes and makeup my mother wore when she went out, back when she used to go out and still had a life. I'm not making that up, she really doesn't have a life. She's always going on about it to make people feel sorry for her: "I have no life. This is no kind of life."

I know I told you before that she was always bringing guys back to the house, but it's not exactly true. She'd like to, I'm sure, but she doesn't. Sometimes she looks at me and I know what she's thinking. Because of me, she isn't a nurse; because of me, she doesn't have a boyfriend; because of me, she doesn't have a big happy family...

Stupid bitch.

...

Her clothes looked good on me, which surprised me. Once I'd gotten over the weirdness of being a carbon copy of my mother, I thought I looked pretty hot.

Anyway.

I was planning on going to a bar or something. Apparently that's where you go to meet people. Some kids were yelling in the park by our building. I watched them for a bit. They were in the sandbox with bare feet. Jerks.

When I was little, my mother never let me go barefoot in the sandbox. Because of syringes. But yeah, we've talked about that already, I won't go on about it. I wanted to shout out of the window at them: *Don't you have any parents? Get out of the sandbox!*

The magic was working: with the grown-up makeup and clothes, I'd already turned into an old bitch.

The only problem was shoes. My feet are really small but my mother's are normal size. So I couldn't wear hers. And it's pretty obvious that a clingy dress with Adidas and socks isn't a good look. So do you know what I did?

I grabbed the sexiest high heels I could find in her closet

and took them with me. My feet were bare, and I held the shoes by the straps, to pretend like my feet were hurting so much that I'd had to take my shoes off. That came to me because of those kids earlier. See, you're thinking I'm giving you irrelevant details, but you realize later that they are actually relevant.

Anyway, it was a shitty idea.

The more I walked and the darker it got, the more I got stressed out about treading on a syringe. Okay, I admit I'm a bit obsessed. It's my crazy mother's fault for passing her neuroses on to me. Every time my heel landed on a small sharp stone I said to myself, "Now look what's happened, I'm going to die."

Because AIDS isn't exactly a fun way to go, you know? My mother told me about it when I was little to frighten me.

So I freaked out. I sat down on a low wall, and I swear, if I'd been the kind of girl who cries, I would've been crying right then. I could be an adult, sure, but only if I could have the right shoes, you know?

So then this car stopped. And if a car stops at night in my neighbourhood, you're not going to wait around to see what they want, because it's probably not going to be some nice nun wanting to know the way to the Santiago de Compostela. It was Jo or Mel, one or the other, who said that. I don't remember which one. No, it wasn't my mother. My mother said, "Aicha, I mean it, I don't even want to think about you being outside after dark."

I obeyed her. She'll never have to think about it.

So anyway, there I am sitting on my little wall and this car stops right in front of me. *What could possibly happen to me that's worse than stepping on a syringe?* I thought. I went up to the car door and saw it was the brother of some guy at my school, I can't remember his name. The guy's or his brother's.

He said, "Do you know who I am? I'm Whatsit. Thingy's brother. Where are you going? Want a ride?"

I got in. He asked me where I was going again.

I really had no idea where I was going, so I asked him if he was too young to drive. He said, "Yup, and you're too young to go out dressed like that." He leaned over and frenched me. I let him.

I hadn't really even made out with anyone before. Except for my hand, standing in for Baz, when I'm in bed at night. I don't know if he was a bad kisser or if I was the one who sucked, but he nearly suffocated me with his tongue. I had spit all over me, plus his three beard hairs were scratching me.

Well, looks like my first time's gonna be pretty sucky, I thought. He put his hands under my dress and he wasn't even gentle. It hurt when he stuck two fingers straight in. Nothing like when I do it myself. I tried to imagine that he was Baz, but it was impossible. Baz would never do it like that anyway.

When *he* touches me it's soft, slippery. It's sweet like a strawberry milkshake.

My mind was wandering while Whatsit was fiddling away. Obviously I was thinking of Jo and Mel and their fail-safe ways of not bleeding and for it to be fun when you get taken from behind. It had to be the same for being taken from the front, right?

"Spit on your fingers," I told him.

"Suck me instead," and he took his dick out of his pants.

They're ugly things, aren't they?

I'd seen one before, but when you're about to put one in your mouth I guess you pay a bit more attention than when you just see some junkie who's taken a piss in an alley and forgotten to put it away again.

When I seemed to be hesitating a bit, he grabbed my hair in his hands and pulled my head toward…it.

I wanted to say to him, *Hey, you've been looking at it for sixteen years and you'd never put it in your mouth! Give me two minutes to get myself together.* But then I thought, *Oh, fuck it. It's not like it's going to suddenly turn into a Häagen-Dazs ice cream.*

So I sucked it.

…

Have you ever ended up two blocks away from your house, and three away from the house of the person you love, giving a blow job to some guy you don't know in a stolen car, because the car was actually stolen?

Yeah. I was thinking it was a no too.

Anyway, when you end up two blocks away from your house, and three away from the house of the person you love, giving a blow job to some guy you don't know in a stolen car, loads of stuff go through your head.

Could my jaw actually get dislocated? Or I think we're parked somewhere we might get a ticket or Hey, his wallet is in the cupholder.

All that, and other stuff too.

You're wondering if you're doing it right. Because even if you don't care about the guy in question, you don't want to look like a total loser. At school or to the whole neighbourhood. You don't want to be *that* girl who doesn't even know which end is up. You wanna seem like you know what you're doing. But not like you know *too* much. Otherwise you'll get a reputation as the school skank, and next thing you know some porn director will be calling you up because he's heard of you and wants you to be his "rising star." It happened to a girl I know.

Well, okay, not a girl I *know* know, but a girl that someone I know knows.

Then I started wondering if my mother might find me, or, even worse, Baz!

If worse came to worst, my mother would've gotten so mad I might've almost liked it. Except she'd never have let me go out ever again, and she'd have followed through on her threat to work less so she could look after me. Which would seriously be a disaster.

But just imagine if Baz had walked by.

Fine, so I was doing it because of him, to piss him off and to show him that I was an adult. But I wouldn't have wanted to see him when I had someone else's penis in my mouth. I think I really would have bawled if that had happened.

I wanted to throw up. And it wasn't even anything to do with the blow job, because his dick wasn't even long enough to reach the part that makes you retch. But the more I thought about wanting to throw up, the more I wanted to throw up. And the juice that comes out tastes fucking disgusting, so you can imagine what it was like.

He pulled my hair to stop me. I wanted to ask if it was because I was no good, like on the bus, when the person sitting next to you moves to a different seat and you sniff yourself all over to see if it's you that smells or what. But before I could say anything, he asked me to put my shoes on.

Wow, I'm so pathetic he's gonna throw me out of his car, I thought. How rude, huh? I put on the shoes and showed him they were too big. He didn't seem to give a shit.

Johannie had told me some guys have weird fetishes. If you don't know, a fetish is something that turns you on. His must have been shoes.

His dick was still sticking out of his pants, it was kind of ridiculous. Like that tramp who wanders around the streets beating their boner and snickering. He's so dirty I wonder how he doesn't spray dust everywhere when he jerks off.

I must admit, I really didn't want to do it anymore.

I stared at his thing hanging out and said to myself that it was like jumping into a cold pool. The anticipation is the worst part. Once you're in, it's fine.

It's gross, there are too many people, every time you move you get a ton of hair between your fingers, but it's not that bad.

So I got on top of him, pushed my underwear aside, and boom.

It didn't hurt too much. He had his hands under my skirt, on my ass, and he pushed me up and down on him. Luckily I'd stumbled across a guy who knew more or less how to do it, because I would've just stayed there without moving, waiting for I don't know what. It could have taken a while.

He did the back-and-forth thing fourteen times. After the third time it got a bit boring. On the seventh, it started to sting a bit. By the ninth, it was really hurting. On the twelfth go, I swore I'd never do this again in my life.

On the thirteenth time, I buried my head in his shoulder and said, *Baz...Baz...Baz,* over and over again in my head.

He came inside me, it was running all down my thighs, and it was hot and gross. "Well, thanks, that was fun," he said, before adding, "See you again!" and pretty much falling asleep with his head resting on the window.

I pinched the wallet from the cupholder and got out of the car, forgetting my mother's shoes.

I ran back home with bare feet. I didn't give a shit about stepping on a syringe anymore.

Of course, when I got home, my mother was already there.

She's never there except when I don't want her to be. It's like she invented Murphy's Law.

She started freaking out because I'd borrowed her clothes. "Blah blah blah, where have you been, blah blah blah, what are you wearing..."

I hate her, I hate her, I hate her!

Like I needed that just then, right?

My eye makeup had run a bit. Not because I'd cried, it had just run. My eyes are too wet or something. My mother started screeching at me, wanting to know what was wrong with me. She followed me up to my room, I locked the door, and she stayed outside it talking to me as if I were some fragile little animal or something.

I hate it when people talk to me like I'm a fragile little animal. I'm not a fragile little animal.

Anyway.

I went to bed, and I wanted to bawl, so that my insides would get washed out and all the shit would leave with my tears. And I really wanted to have a shower, so that Whatsit's sperm would stop running down my legs, but that crazy woman was blocking the door. She's a fucking lunatic, I tell you. She does that sometimes. Screams and then comes and presses herself against my door. She thinks I listen to her babbling on about how she would really love it if I loved her, and how she doesn't know what she did wrong with me and she really wants me to tell her about it and blah blah blah.

That time, like I just said, she wanted to know what I'd been doing, where I'd been and everything. Not so she could yell at me, just to know. "It's for your own good, I just want to protect you, Aicha."

Yeah, right.

Bitch.

The last time she just wanted to protect me, Hakim went off without me and never came back.

Normally I don't bother replying when she goes off on one of her rants about how she's such a victim. I just sing in my head, or count how many ninety-degree angles there are in my room. But right then I had so many things I wanted to get out that I just couldn't hold back.

You know when a boat's sinking, like in movies, the captain tries to plug the holes with anything he can get his hands on, but the water comes in anyway.

Well, it was just like that, except that it was trying to get out, not in, obviously.

Fine, *I* know what I mean anyway.

I yelled at her what I just said to you: "Last time you just wanted to protect me, Hakim took off and he never came back!"

Silence. Like it took her a moment to absorb the blow. I felt the shock wave through the door. Everything went, like, muted. Heavy.

If I hadn't felt so bad once I said it, I'd be pretty proud of hitting the mark. I seriously sent her spinning. She was so not expecting that!

But as for me, it was like someone had peeled off all my skin and then dumped a load of salt on me. I could just about manage to think that I needed to go take a shower to wash off all the salt. But it wasn't even real, it was imaginary salt. Anyway, you know what I mean.

I was imagining washing myself like a cat. Like licking myself and then rubbing. But that seemed too gross.

She said really quietly, "But, Aicha, he was abusing you, he was a piece of shit."

I wanted to kill her.

You know when you feel like you're leaving your body behind, that there's so much rage in it that there's no room left for you? That's how it felt. I cried hard for a long time.

"If he was my real father, he wouldn't have done it. But because you're such a slut, you cheated on him, got pregnant with me, and here we are. It's all your fault. Everything is your fault. You're the one who should've left, we didn't need you." I smashed a couple of things.

I heard her banging furiously on my door. "If I open this door, I'm going to kill you!" I said when she asked me to open it.

I'm serious, I tell you. I would have killed her.

She calmed down finally and gave up the idea of coming into my room.

She was still crying on the other side of the door. *Who exactly do you think's gonna feel sorry for you?* I was thinking.

After that, she blubbered about how she wanted to explain

things to me blah blah blah. But I already knew everything she wanted to tell me. I know all her bullshit.

She started telling me a load of crap, so I put on some music to drown her out.

I'm not going to tell you her side of the story.

You'll just have to ask her.

And then you know what'll happen? She's the one you'll believe. Because she plays the victim really fucking well.

She'll tell you Hakim was just a loser who was pissing his life away and cheating on her and living off her money, and that she was working like four people, poor her, just to keep us alive. She'll tell you she never cheated on him, that she left because it couldn't last, and then she fucked someone else, except she won't say "fucked." But she was still living with Hakim because she couldn't throw him out because my mother's a fucking saint, you know, and apparently she still loved him and thought he was going to change blah blah blah.

Except then she got pregnant and here we are. She thought it was Hakim's, but it was the other guy's, who came from I don't even know where and I don't wanna know.

I seriously don't give a shit about my real father.

Well, okay, it's true I don't give a shit, but every time I see a guy who's blond like me in the street and is around my mother's age, I wonder if he could be the one.

I don't know what that does to me. It doesn't do anything to me. It's just a thought that passes.

Anyway.

See how crazy she is and how she can turn everything to her advantage?

In any case, you go question her, and you'll see what she says. Exactly what I've just said.

Then she'll explain how and why she kicked him out the house. She shut me in my room, the bitch, because she knew I'd leave with him if she let me out.

She told him that if he ever came near me again she'd call the police.

Do you see how sick she is?

It still hurts when I think about it.

Sometimes I still hope he'll come back and find me and then we'll go somewhere far away. Far away from her, far away from syringes on the ground, far away from the cops, far away from all this shit... Maybe I've said that already. I used to think about it every night before I went to sleep, but ever since I met Baz I don't think about it so much.

I don't want to talk about it. If Hakim really was abusing me and all that shit.

I don't want to.

Why do you want a break? I don't care if it's lunchtime. I'm not hungry.

At the beginning, I said I'd tell you everything you wanted to know because I knew everyone would just leave me alone after that.

I just want to be left alone.

…

You want to know if Hakim was abusing me? I'll tell you, I really don't care.

Because no.

I've had the chance to think back, over time, you know. I even looked up *abuse* in the dictionary tons of times. In all the dictionaries that exist, I think.

I know what abuse means, it means rape. I know what rape is. I even almost got raped one time, nearly. That's how I met Baz.

But I've already told you that story.

That has nothing to do with Hakim and me. He wasn't some old drunk hiding out in the park. He was good-looking and I loved him.

That's why my mother threw him out. Because she was jealous. That's the real reason. The sad truth.

But you'll never see that in the *Journal de Montréal*. No, no, no. If my story was ever in the paper, the headline wouldn't be "Cruel, Jealous Mother Falsely Accuses Boyfriend and Wrecks Child's Life." It would be "Model Mother Saves Her Beloved Daughter from PEDOPHILE'S"—all caps, of course—"Clutches. He's Still at Large. Hide Your Children. Be Afraid!"

Anyway.

Do you know what the worst part is?

The worst part is, one time I heard my mother on the phone to her friend, and she said, "He's broken my daughter, completely broken her, Anouk. If I ever see him again I'll kill him with my bare hands. And you know I'm the least violent person ever."

Of course she was talking about him. You know how sometimes people accuse other people of things to hide their own mistakes? I read that in *Elle* once. But you're like a psychologist. You must have learned that kind of thing in psychology school, right?

It's called a transfer, or something like that. You break something and afterwards you say, "No, he broke it, not me."

So no, Hakim wasn't abusing me. We hugged and kissed and everything but it was fun.

I don't give a shit if you think that's gross.

…

We used to watch a million movies when I wasn't at school. He would say to me, "Hey, kiddo, wanna go and get me a beer?" I'd go, and I'd get another one out of the fridge at the same time, because he liked his beer not too cold, but not warm either. A bit colder than tepid. Getting the beer the right temperature for Hakim was a science, and I was so fucking good at it. My mother wasn't. She didn't give a shit, she just told him he could get his own beer. For me it was like a vocation. I could have spent my life doing that. "I'm so happy you're here," he used to say to me, giving me a kiss. "You're the perfect woman."

Do you know what it means to be a perfect woman?

Has anyone ever told you you're a perfect woman?

I'd be surprised, actually, I mean, you're not exactly beautiful. So you probably don't know what it feels like. It's like an amazing caress, everywhere on your body and inside at the same time. Imagine if all the pores of your skin were eating something really good…

I mean, sure, that's not even possible, but just pretend.

…

Or when you're snuggling with someone you love on the couch, watching one of the best movies ever made, even if you don't really understand what they're saying in it apart from "You're the disease and I'm the cure."

That's not *Scarface*, that's *Cobra*.

Yeah, I didn't think you were gonna know that one either.

Anyway, watching it while being stroked by a thumb you love.

At first it was just a thumb. On the hip. You snuggle up closer and it turns into all the fingertips.

You're not watching the movie at all anymore, but that's no problem because you've already seen it dozens and dozens of times.

You're only thinking about how the more you turn around, the better it is. The closer his fingers come to your...thing, the more pleasure and electricity you feel inside. And everything goes slowly.

You don't know if it's okay to turn around too quickly. It's kind of forbidden, but you don't really know why. Maybe because people always ban things that feel good.

You snuggle up closer because you want to get inside his body.

Sometimes you move a bit too much and he moves his hand away. Then you come back to reality with a bump. You want to shout, you want to take his hand and put it back where it was.

But you don't dare.

You never dare.

After a while, he does put his hand back. You've got your head on his chest, you can't even hear the TV anymore, you really don't give a shit about the movie anymore. You can hear his heart beating faster and faster, and louder. Sometimes that's the point where he gets hard. Sometimes it's later on, when you turn over on your back, pretending it's not deliberate, and his hand slides from your hip to your belly. Or even lower.

Touching your underwear, between your legs. Very gently. As if he was petting a baby bird.

He asks if that feels good, but you don't dare answer, because you can't really admit that you like something forbidden. You just say, "Mmm-mmm." He says that he likes it too. He asks you to look at the effect it's had on him. You can touch it if you want.

But you don't dare.

Because, like I said before, you never dare.

When you like a guy, it gets really tricky. You can give a blow job to the brother of some guy from school, hop on top and fuck him, play the slut as much as you want, but when you love someone, you can't do anything, you're just paralyzed. It's even worse when you're nine than when you're thirteen.

That's how it is. It's shit, but that's how it is.

And when he leaves because your crazy mother throws him out of the house because she's jealous of you, you tell yourself that maybe if you'd dared, he would have stayed.

Or maybe he'd have come back to find you.

Anyway.

Are you even listening to me, or are you just opening your eyes super wide and giving me juice with fucking pulp in it?

If I knew where Hakim was, do you really think I'd be here now?

Okay, yeah, maybe I'd be here, but anyway. You know what I mean. Or you don't. Sometimes it feels like I'm talking to you in a foreign language. But it's not just you. It's everyone. That's why I don't have any friends. Sometimes it's not just a different language, it's like I belong to a whole different species. You know how when you talk to a dog, it doesn't understand you... Well, maybe not a dog, because dogs are really good at English, but let's say a cat.

I fucking hate cats.

Dogs understand what you're saying, and they're always willing to do what you want, whatever it is. If you say, "Wanna go for a walk?" they're as happy as if you'd said, "Wanna go to church and be bored out of your mind?" I mean, just for example. I've never actually said that to a dog. I just wanted to show you how accommodating dogs are compared with cats. Well, compared with anything, really.

I'd like to have a dog. Any dog, I don't care. But it has to be good-looking. And big.

But I don't want a cat. Cats are stupid, just like people. They understand what you're saying but they just don't care. They never want to come and do stuff with you except when you don't want them to. Like when you're going to the bathroom or whatever. You don't want to be watched by a pair of eyes and be judged on how bad it stinks and how long it's taking you. That's what cats do. They're always there between your legs when you don't need them, just to get in your way. And they judge you. And they think the sun shines out of their asses, even though they lick them.

Anyway, I can't really blame them for that because I know tons of humans who would think the sun shone out of their asses if they could lick them too.

I can't even remember why I was telling you that.

The kind of dog I'd really like is a cross between a Rottweiler and a German shepherd. The squeegee kid at the corner of Ontario and Iberville, the one with the face tattoos who's going out with the girl with holes in her tights and a pit bull, he has one.

I petted him once. The dog, not the squeegee kid.

…

It's hard to tell with you, maybe you suddenly think I'm walking the streets petting old punks. He is cool though.

But not enough that I want to pet him. His dog's name is Sid.

Like Sid Vicious. Do you know who that is?

Really?

You amaze me.

I'm hungry after all.

No, I don't want anything.

I'm hungry, but I don't want to eat.

There's a knot in my stomach.

And anyway, if you brought me, let's say, a ham sandwich, you'd get the extra-fat kind, it would make me blow chunks, and I already feel like puking.

It really irritates me when people say, "You just feel nauseous because you're hungry." That's your kind of thing, isn't it? It's my mother's too. Her kind of thing. Whatever.

I'd really like to see Baz. Can we go and see him? Not for long, just five minutes. I wouldn't talk to him, I just wanna see him.

…

Please?

Where is he? Come on, tell me. I just want to see him for five minutes, I'm not going to touch him, I'm not going to talk to him, I promise.

Please…

…

I'm not crying, I don't want a tissue. I want to see Baz. And after that I'll tell you everything you want to know.

At least tell me when I'll be able to see him.

Please!

…

Why are you so mean? Why won't you take me to see him? I'm not going to tell you anything else until I've seen him.

…

Couldn't we go to wherever he is, and you put him in a room with, like, one of those two-way mirrors, and I'll be on the other side, and that way you'll know I can't talk to him?

I'd just put my hand on the glass and look at him. Please, just five minutes. Two minutes!

Take me to see him. You can even stay in the room, I don't care. I have the right! I know I have the right!

And he has the right too, he can ask for it. I'm sure he must have asked.

Tell him I want to see him. Call him wherever he is and tell him.

Fine, if you want me to beg, I'll beg.

Just a tiny minute…

…

You are such a bitch.

I've been telling you my whole life story all this time, and then I ask you one thing and you won't even do it. I don't give a shit, I'm not going to tell you anything else, never again, it's over. And I take back everything I've said. Anyway, I've been lying the whole time, none of what I've told you is true. You can delete everything.

From now on, I can't remember anything and I'm going to keep my trap shut until the moment you tell Baz that I'm fine, and then take me to see him.

…

I don't even want to touch him, I don't even want to talk to him…

Please.

…

Please.

Accusations?

Yeah, no!

That's what I've been trying to make you see this whole time, he didn't do anything. I know he didn't! I swear he didn't do anything.

I'll carry on telling you everything that happened, like the *true* true story, then I'll go and find him, and then you'll never hear from us ever again. Okay?

Can I see him and tell him that? Just to reassure him and so he knows everything's gonna be okay?

Can you tell him where I am, tell him everything's gonna be okay?

…

I don't feel good, everything's spinning. I'm going to sit back down again, I think. Okay?

Okay.

…

Could you open the window? Open the window. I'm suffocating. I need to get out. I might be dying. I'm going to suffocate and die. Open the window. I'm hot.

Don't come near me, just…open the window.

If you don't open the window, I'm going to die, that's what's gonna happen.

…

I need to go and sit over there in the corner. I don't need long, I'm just going…over there.

…

No, I can't. I don't want to. There are people outside, it's too big, everything's spinning. Just…I'm suffocating, I'm for real going to die, I'm all itchy and hot.

…

Let go of me.

I'm sick, let go of me. Let go of me.

I'm gonna barf.

…

No, stay here. I need you to stay here otherwise nobody will know if I suffocate. And I'm gonna suffocate pretty soon, I can tell.

Don't go away, don't come near me. If you come near me I'm going to go crazy, I swear. That's what's gonna happen.

…

Don't touch me.

…

I'm hot, I don't feel good, I'm suffocating. Let me go.

I'm gonna die.

…

Keep your hand on my head. Don't move.

…

Yes.

…

Okay.

…

I'm gonna throw up. For real.

…

I can't breathe anymore, for real, I swear.

...

It hurts.

...

It hurts.

I'm sorry, I didn't mean to throw up on you just then.

Are you mad?

I'd be fucking furious.

But it's good you had stuff to change into, so it's not too bad.

Do you have, like, your own showers, or are they the same as ours, so you barely want to stick a toe in because they're full of old hair, dried soap, mould, and warts?

...

I've been itchy ever since I had a shower. I'm sure I picked up some horrible flesh-eating bacteria from standing on a gob of spit. Is that even possible?

Nobody takes me seriously anyway. It's become like a joke every time I say I'm gonna die. Not necessarily *die* die, just...

There are some seriously gross diseases, you have no idea. Does your mother work in a hospital? So you don't know about all the things you could catch. And believe me, you don't wanna know. I know, and it totally freaks me out.

But only when I think about it.

"Whenever you think about it, just stop thinking about it," Baz used to tell me. That's number twenty-four on my list of reasons why I love him. He says things like that. It's pretty hot, right? He can actually pretend there's nothing wrong and just go on living normally. Supervolcanoes, flesh-eating bacteria, particle accelerators, and all that kind of crap, it doesn't bother him.

You know when something makes you freak out, and I mean like seriously freak out, you're suffocating and you end up actually being sick, kinda like just now, and someone's next to you trying to make you believe it's nothing serious, but not like, "Come on, you silly goose, you're just freaking out about crap," but just like using the energy they're giving off so you just know everything's gonna be alright. Even if everything's going to shit around you, even if you're being attacked from all sides, even if it seems like the world's gonna end, or your lactose intolerance is gonna kill you.

That's just the kind of guy he is. Like a desert island where you wash up after a huge fucking storm. But with food and water and all that on it. And a house with heating. And Internet.

Okay, maybe that wasn't a good example.

Like yesterday, if he hadn't been there, I think I would have been totally messed up.

…

But I don't wanna tell you about all that right away, okay?

I promise I'll tell you everything. Just not right away. You need to understand stuff first. What we had together, me and him. I want you to know everything so it's almost like you're in my head.

You really need to understand it's not his fault at all, everything that happened. He didn't do anything. Afterwards, you can explain everything to the cops and they'll let him go.

And me…

Will I go to prison?

What's going to happen to me?

…

Can I call my mother?

I'd like to see her.

…

When I tell you about how Baz is like a house or something cool like that, well, with her it's just the opposite. You didn't see her when they called her yesterday. She didn't have a clue about what was going on, all she could do was cry.

And that's useless when there's a crisis. All she can do is bawl and bawl, and then when you think she's done she bawls some more.

But still, it would be cool if she was here.

…

Okay.

Anyway, I hadn't finished telling you earlier. There are so many things, I don't even know what I've started, it's confusing.

You know that business with the brother of the guy from school, in the car? I know the car was stolen because before I got out I jacked the wallet in the cupholder.

No joke, there was at least two thousand bucks in it. I wanted to give it back but in the end I told myself the guy shouldn't have gotten his car stolen. He must have been a douche anyway. Who goes around with two thousand bucks in their car, except for a pimp?

And I looked at his cards. He had a face like a pimp.

The next day I bought a ton of clothes and an iPod. And a big leather bracelet for Baz at H&M. There were so many other things I wanted to buy him but I didn't know what size he was. The bracelet was one size fits all so I knew it would work.

I showed up at his place with all my bags and then he started in with all his questions.

"What are all these clothes?" "Where did you get the money to buy all this stuff?" "Aren't you a bit young to wear something like that?"

I pretended not to hear him, and I asked him if he wanted me to try on my new things and show him. He said, "Um…," so I pretended to sulk until he said yes.

Out of all those clothes, my favourite thing was a black dress. He said, "Yeah, that's kinda sexy!" or something. He also wanted to know what had happened to me overnight, so I told him about fucking the guy in the car.

Well, I didn't actually say "in the car" or anything, I sugar-coated it a bit, you know. Jo told me to make him jealous. She didn't know it was him, she thought it was some guy in my class at school. Like I'd be interested in some guy in my class! Anyway, she told me to make him jealous, so that's what I did.

At least, that's what I tried to do. I don't really know if it worked. I don't know what a jealous guy looks like, so maybe he was but I didn't notice.

When I asked him, he said he wasn't. But it's gotta be the kind of thing like when you're sad. If someone asks you if you're sad you just say, "No, I've just got something in my eye," or "No, you stupid bitch, it's my allergies."

That night there was a party at his place, so he said I couldn't stay because there'd be alcohol and stuff.

I sulked, I insisted, but he didn't want me to stay.

So I left feeling really mad and hoping he'd run after me in the street, but he's not really the kind of guy who'd do that.

I went to see old Klop at the convenience store to chat a bit. I really like his stories. "Where are you going dressed like that?" he said.

I said, "Precisely nowhere, because there's a party that's gonna be really cool at this guy's house who I really like, but I'm not invited."

Klop said if the guy hadn't invited me, he didn't deserve me loving him.

I nearly said, "Oh, you don't get it at all, you jerk," but I didn't say it because he's still kind, even if he has no clue about what goes on in the real world with real people.

He gave me a KitKat.

I felt super bad about calling him a jerk in my head. So I asked him to tell me the story of how he won the store by playing cards in whatever decade it was, I can't even remember, because he likes telling that one. It changes a bit every time, so it's not like he's repeating himself.

That night my mother was working the night shift, or at least she wasn't home. Her schedule's on the fridge in case I need it, or in case I give a fuck, but since that isn't the case, I never look at it.

I fell asleep on the couch. I made myself some nachos, they were pretty awesome, but nachos always put me to sleep, so it was like 3:00 a.m. when I woke up.

I wasn't tired anymore, so I went to Baz's place to see if there were still lights on.

The lights were on and the door was open.

He was in the middle of tidying up. There were like tons and tons of bottles and cans everywhere, and full ashtrays, and the floor was all sticky. And it stank.

It was super depressing.

I just said, "Hello," from the doorway. I didn't know if I had the right to be there, if he was still mad or what…

…

Yeah…

…

Well, I guess I didn't quite tell it right before.

It didn't really happen like I said. He got, like, annoyed at one point, I can't really remember why.

…

Okay, wow.

So you cut me off and then you make stuff up? That's not good.

When I tell you I can't remember, it's because I can't remember. Do you think I'm lying or what?

…

It was almost like I told you: I was trying on my clothes, I came to the black dress, and he said something like, "Um…that's kinda sexy for someone your age, don't you think?" and I said guys like that. He sighed, then he said he was having a party so I had to leave. I insisted on staying, but he said it wasn't appropriate for people my age, that there was going to be alcohol and that kind of thing so he'd prefer it if I went home.

I said, "You're always banging on about how this and that isn't appropriate for someone my age, but you know what? Yesterday I slept with some guy and I thought it was pretty fun for a thing that's not appropriate for someone my age, so maybe it would be the same thing with alcohol."

He said, "What? What are you talking about? Are you telling the truth?"

I said yes and looked him straight in the eyes. I started

telling him about it but he started freaking out. Going on about how I hadn't understood anything he'd said to me, that that wasn't what he had in mind. He asked me who the guy was.

"Who's the little shit who was brain-dead enough to do that with you? Does he know how old you are? You're really not right in the head, Aicha," he said.

Or something like that.

"Are you jealous?" I said, kind of hopeful.

Apparently that wasn't the right thing to say. It just got him more fired up. I thought it was a legitimate question but apparently not.

He started off, "Yeah, Aicha. Every single guy on the planet who thinks it's sick for a thirteen-year-old girl to get screwed in a stolen car by some guy she doesn't know is jealous. That's right. I'm jealous."

That was sarcasm, by the way, in case you didn't know.

He carried on, "You seemed to understand what I said to you, but didn't you get any of it? When I talk to you, does any of it go in or are you just nodding away like a bobble-head in a car? Fucking hell, Aicha, didn't you want to wait to do that with a guy you actually love? Didn't you want it to mean something? Didn't you want it not to make you feel like throwing up every time you think about it?"

I shot back that if he'd wanted to make love to me, if he was in love with me, if he loved me like he ought to, then it would never have happened.

He said, "Get out."

So I got out.

I went to get a takeout McDonald's meal with what was left of the money from the stolen car guy's wallet, and then I sat down outside Baz's place, not so close to seem stalkerish but close enough to see the door.

At one point I got cold, but it was no big deal because I

had all those clothes in my H&M bags. I felt a bit like a freak, you know, like some homeless person with all their garbage bags piled up in their shopping cart.

But I didn't care.

A party goes on for a long time, hey? The people had barely even started to arrive and I was already bored out of my mind.

So I did go to see old Klop, but he wasn't there. The KitKat part's true, it just didn't happen that day. Jo was with a client and Mel was all mad about some guy who'd insulted her. When she's in that state it's best not to get too close.

I went back to my house and fell asleep in front of the TV with the hole in the screen.

It wasn't planned, I just wanted to chill for a half-hour before going back to keep a lookout at Baz's. In the end I woke up around two-thirty.

There was still music playing at his place, but quieter than when I'd gone by on my way back from the convenience store. It was a bit of a detour but it's not like I had anything else to do.

I got there right when some people were leaving. They were totally drunk and kept asking me if I wasn't kinda late showing up, how old I was, and all that. I gave them the finger but I felt bad about it afterwards because maybe they were really good friends of Baz's, and it's always good to be friends with your boyfriend's friends.

But anyway, what's done is done.

I waited at the top of the stairs for the last guests to leave.

There was just one person left.

It was a girl. I couldn't get a good look at her but she seemed fat and ugly.

"I'm so happy I met you," she was saying.

"Me too," he replied.

"See you soon, I hope," she said, laughing like some fat ugly turkey.

I couldn't breathe, the same way it happened just now. I thought I was going to die then too. It took me a good half-hour to feel normal again.

After that I went inside, because I thought he was going to bed and I just wanted to…I dunno. Be with him. See him.

I don't know.

He was in the middle of clearing up. It took him a few minutes to notice I was there. It was so cute, he was tripping and stumbling all over the place, and talking to things. Hakim used to do that too when he'd had too much to drink.

He jumped when he saw me.

I said, "I'm sorry about before."

He sat down on the couch and patted the spot next to him for me to join him. He put his arms around me and said he was the one who was sorry. He stroked my hair and dropped a kiss on the top of my head…

Usually I hate that, but this time it was different.

He asked me if I could understand why he couldn't do anything. I said no. He laughed a bit. He said, "I'd smash that guy's face in. I was thinking about it all night. I feel sick that he had his dirty hands on you. That he kissed you…"

"Well, technically he didn't really even touch me. I was the one who—"

"I don't want to hear about it, Aicha, please, stop with the details. It seriously makes me want to throw up. I just want to stop thinking about it."

"So stop! Think about something else instead!"

That was a little in-joke about what I was telling you about before, but he didn't get it.

"I can't! I've drunk three times as much as I should have, all my friends were here, this whole night with the music and the girls, and the only thing I could think about was you and him. Why did you do that? Please tell me it wasn't because of me."

You know sometimes when time stops and you're just, like, watching what's happening? It was like that then.

I was watching it and thinking, *Wow, it's happening for real. It really is.*

I said, "I love you, Baz, and I want to be with you." Then I kissed him.

He resisted a bit to begin with, but I could tell he wanted to. He said my name twice, and hearing it just made me so happy. I love the way he says "Aicha."

He kisses really well. Perfectly. I don't have too much to compare him with, but I can tell you he's the best kisser in the world. He was holding me tightly against him, his hands were in my hair and on my back…

I wanted him, you can't even imagine. I could have carried on kissing him like that for hours, but I was afraid my belly would explode with wanting him so much. I asked him to say my name again. Making love with someone who knows your name is pretty cool. He was stroking my hair and kissing me all over my face and neck. I undid his belt. He said, "Hold on, Aicha, no…"

I asked him if he wanted to, and said that I did too. And then I said, "If you make love to me, it'll be my first time."

He carried me to the bed, still kissing me, and undressed me. We laughed a bit because the dress, the same one, was really sexy but not that easy to get off. I helped him take off his sweater, his jeans, and his boxers. I looked at him for a long time and thought he was really hot. Everywhere. Even completely naked I thought he was hot. He lay on top of me, between my legs. He wasn't even heavy, it didn't squish me like I thought it was going to. We kissed a bit more, but I wanted him so bad I couldn't even appreciate his kisses anymore. I opened my legs as wide as I could, I put my hands on his ass, and I said, "Baz, I can't wait anymore, I want you so bad it hurts."

He entered me super gently. My pleasure was going more

off the charts with every inch.

It was good, it was so good!

I cried, it was so good.

I kept saying, "Baz, Baz, Baz," and he kept saying, "Aicha! Oh, Aicha!"

He came on my stomach. I would've liked him to come inside me but it was still good.

He put his arms around me and went to sleep.

I didn't sleep, I was playing with the sperm around my belly button. *It's because it's his that it doesn't seem gross to me,* I thought.

I licked my fingers.

I was smiling like an idiot and trying to press up against him as much as I could. All my skin against his skin.

I was so happy.

The girl on the stairs?

I don't know who she was, I didn't get a good look at her.

…

Okay, fine, it was her.

What a sucky name, right? Élisanne Blais.

It's not even a real name. It's like a bit of Élise and a bit of Anne, but not really either. It's like two half names that don't make one nice one even when you join them together. And Blais sounds like Bleugh!

"Would you care for some more sauerkraut, Élisanne?"

"Bleugh!"

Whatever.

Yeah, go right ahead and look at me like, *If I were you I wouldn't be laughing at other people's names with your Arabic name and your blond hair and blue eyes,* but it's not the same thing. Mine's like a style thing. It's not the same. Anyway, I don't give a shit.

I wouldn't go to parties and try to pick up other people's boyfriends with my fat ugly face. I just wouldn't do that.

No kidding, I was watching her talk to Baz in the doorway, and I was sending her subliminal messages like *Fuck off, you fat cow,* but she wasn't receiving the telepathy, she was just sticking around like gum on the bottom of your shoe. You know, like when you have to get it off with a knife or a stick because otherwise your foot sticks to the floor every time you take a step, and it's as annoying as fuck?

Anyway.

There she was chatting away and telling him her whole life story, and she was standing there telling him she was so happy to have met him and all that crap… Like obviously she was happy to have met him! It's like if I met Tony Montana, for example. I'd be happy, but I wouldn't go on about it, because he'd just say, "Of course you're happy, babe, I'm Tony Montana."

Same thing. When you meet Baz your life changes and gets better, you're happy, but you don't say it. You pick up your shit and you get the fuck out of there.

Because he's mine.

…

By the way, you know I know Tony Montana isn't real, right? It's just an example, I'm not completely stupid. But I just wanted to compare it with someone you'd understand. Because objectively speaking there aren't that many people as cool as Baz who really exist. But you wouldn't know that because you don't know him.

…

Sometimes I think your life must be super boring.

I don't wanna talk about Élisanne Blais.

Not right now.

I told you I'd tell you everything but not right away. I can't remember anyway.

Why do we have to talk about her?

It's super annoying.

My mom's mom's mom was called Nana, and she was a mean old crazy bitch. And I'm talking objectively, right, not just according to my standards. Everyone thought so, even my mother.

We went to see her in France one time, when my mother was still talking to her family.

She used to pinch me.

I swear it's true. She pinched my thighs and then my arm fat and everything.

I don't remember it, but people told me about it, or I heard some conversation between I don't even know who.

She was the kind of old lady who buried babies alive in her garden. Or worse, drowned puppies or kittens.

Kittens aren't quite as bad, because at the end of the day they're just cats, and I hate cats, but still… They're cute when they're little but then they just dump you. I'd never drown kittens, ever.

But Nana, she totally would.

So she was a crazy old whore.

And you know what? When she died, nobody danced on her grave, nobody spat in her coffin, nobody said, "Yay! The old bitch has croaked!" Everyone was saying, "Oh, it's so sad Nana died."

If I'd known that she'd pinched me, or that she called me the little bastard, I would've taken a shit on her grave. I wouldn't even have *put* her in a grave. I would've left her out to rot on a stake, so the pigeons could eat her eyes and the rats could gobble up her guts, the old slut.

...

But I can't even remember why I was telling you that.

Oh yeah. Because I hate that when someone dies, right away that person becomes cool, and everyone talks about them, but when she was alive, she was just some scumbag we wanted to forget even existed.

I don't know why people do that. Maybe so they don't feel guilty about having wanted her to die. Or so their ghost doesn't bug them, or whatever. But then, Nana was just the kind of person who'd come back from the dead to terrorize you, so in her case I get it.

Élisanne Blais was a nobody while she was alive and she'll be a nobody when she's dead. She's not the type to wake you up at 3:13 tapping out a message in Morse code on the wall between your bedroom and the dining room. I'm not scared of Élisanne Blais.

If you wanna talk about her, don't expect me to say she was beautiful, that she was nice, and that everyone loved her and "it's so sad that she's not with us anymore" because it's not true.

Go on, ask away. What do you wanna know about her?

I've already told you she was a bitch, and ugly, and boring, so you know pretty much all there is to know. And you already know that Baz is the most amazing guy on the planet. So automatically, if you're not too stupid, you should be able to reach the same conclusion as me.

…

So, Élisanne Blais had no chance with Baz right from the start. Even with her big soft tits. Even fluttering her eyelashes and saying, "I'm so happy to have met you blah blah blah." I didn't see it coming.

At all.

I was played like a total beginner. I mean, I am a beginner so it's understandable, but still. I've seen loads of movies, I should've known she'd be hanging around to wreck my life. With her big tits and everything.

…

Baz couldn't be dating *her*, with her long brown curly hair right out of a commercial, and her skinny little waist that made her ass look eight times bigger than, well, a normal ass, I guess.

And you should have seen how she wagged her ass when she walked. Swing to the right, swing to the left. Like the whole fucking city was hanging from her ass, like she was on a podium or something. Little Miss I-think-I'm-a-star-and-I-walk-around-like-I-own-the-place.

Anyway.

…

I don't know what else to tell you about her. Except there's no way Baz could be in love with her because he's in love with me, even if he doesn't want to be. He just latched on to the first person his own age so he could pretend he didn't love me.

Yeah.

Deep down, he didn't want her for her tits or her hair or her ass, he just wanted her because of the year she was born. Nothing else. I'm a hundred per cent certain.

You didn't answer me before. Is my mother coming or not?

Not that I give a fuck if she's freaking out, but she must be freaking out.

I was going to see a show with her tomorrow. Do you think I'll be able to go? For her birthday, she said she wanted to have a nice evening, just the two of us. She even asked me if there was anything I wanted to go and see.

I don't know what got into me, I wanted to make her happy. A moment of weakness, I guess.

I went back home, the other time, and I didn't know she was there, because I never look at the schedule she keeps on the fridge, like I said before.

I woke her up when I knocked a shelf over, then two or three other things in my room. I didn't do it deliberately. It made me super mad so I cried a bit, and then she came in and tried to calm me down.

Usually I just get more annoyed if she does that because I don't need her or anything. But just then I hated too many people and too many things were getting on my nerves. I needed all my energy for being miserable and angry, so I went along with it.

And honestly, my mother might be a stupid bitch and all, but what she said made sense. Like she understood I was angry and I needed to let it all out, but that it wouldn't help anybody if I smashed my room up, because I'd only be punishing myself because it was my own things I was breaking.

Yup.

I didn't break everything on purpose, but maybe just a bit.

…

Sometimes that happens to me when I'm really mad. I've always done it. It helps me let off steam.

I don't really know how to explain what happened with my mother then. You know when people say it was just a moment of madness, like when a guy cheats on his wife and that's his excuse?

I get it.

Right then, with my mother, it was a moment of madness. When you've spent your whole life making a path for yourself to follow, you owe it to yourself to stay in a straight line, that's what defines you, that's what makes you who you are… And then a ton of crap happens to you and you get, like, exhausted. And I mean seriously exhausted. Exhausted like there's no more life left inside you. You've been drained of all your blood, your water, and everything that makes you you. You're so empty, your organs are the only thing left inside. Your heart's still beating just to, like, taunt you.

You wanna die, it would be restful, but no. It carries on beating, the bastard, and with each beat you get even more exhausted, it's like torture. You want to beg, but there's nobody to beg. You could ask God to stop messing around with you, but that's assuming he answers requests, or he, like, even exists.

So it makes sense that when you're in that state, hating your mother is the last of your worries.

That's what it was. A moment of madness. A moment of weakness.

We hugged.

She hugged me; I just submitted to it.

I was feeling so shit and discouraged and all the rest of it, it almost seemed cool. Not cool like cool, cool like restful.

…

Now that I think about it, I think I even called her Mom.

She hugged me hard, really hard. So hard that I thought, *Here we go, she's caught me and now she's going to make me pay for all the shit I've put her through, she's gonna murder me. And when they find me dead she'll plead legitimate defence. Or maybe she'll hide her crime by chopping me into little pieces and dumping me in her tomato plants, and when people start wondering where I am, she'll say I ran away, or Hakim came for me and I went off with him and good riddance.*

Do you know what the worst thing is?

The worst thing is that nobody would look for me if my mother chopped me up into little pieces and fertilized her plants with me. I was thinking that the whole time she was squeezing me so hard.

Baz wouldn't look for me, because, you know, we really fought, that's why I lost it so badly, and he basically said he didn't want to see me anymore, all because of that other bitch.

No, not my mother. The *other* bitch, I said.

Anyway. So I was thinking that even *he* wouldn't come looking for me.

Mel and Jo spend their time telling me I shouldn't be hanging out in the streets, that I ought to find myself some friends my own age blah blah blah, so they'd just think I'd listened to them and they wouldn't be worried about me.

Old Klop doesn't remember me from one time I set foot in his store to the next, so I don't think…

No.

Nobody would look for me.

But you know what? Let's say it was somebody other than my mother who was chopping me up and putting me into their flowerpots. I'm sure *she'd* start to wonder where I was.

Thinking about that was kind of disturbing.

I cried and cried and cried, I cried so much that it was hard to tell if it was snot or tears or blood flowing when I rubbed my eyes.

I would've liked to cry tears of blood right then, I admit. But no, it was just snot. Or tears. It was hard to tell, like I told you.

It wasn't just the stuff with Baz, it was everything together, all at the same time. Thirteen years of shit.

Hakim taking off, everyone at school hating me, the old bitch Nana who called me a little bastard, the guy in the stolen car, my mother…my mother…

It doesn't seem like much to you, thirteen years—you must be like a thousand years old or something—but to me it's like my whole life.

A whole life is a really long time, even if it's only thirteen years.

…

Anyway, she asked me if I'd got into such a state because of her, if there was anything she could do. I wanted to say, *Come off it, you're not the centre of the fucking world, you insignificant bitch,* but I was still so lacking in energy and lifeblood that I just had to stay in her arms. So I said, "No." But I did nod when she wondered if it was to do with a boy.

She reeled off some crap about guys and girls… Like if a boy can't see how fantastic I am he doesn't deserve me, that kind of bullshit.

She said we should go out to a restaurant and then the movies on her next day off blah blah blah, I don't even know what else, to raise my spirits.

I don't see how that would have raised my spirits. Especially since her next day off—according to the schedule I never look at—was ages away.

My mother: expert in arriving after the fire and putting it out with a bucket of piss.

I still said yes though. Or at least nodded.

She seemed happy.

She got up off the floor, because we were sitting on the floor, and then she said she was going to make me some mac and cheese. That made me happy. Because it's super annoying but she makes the best mac and cheese in the world.

Anyway.

She said, "I love you, Aicha," and she seemed to really believe it.

For a couple of seconds I felt like I could do anything. You know, all that lack of energy I was telling you about before had totally disappeared. I'd got a boost like when Mario touches a star.

Like I was invincible. So I made the most of it and went back to see Baz.

…

Like I said before, Baz and I argued that night. All because of that fucking Élisanne Blais.

I really feel like you aren't listening to a word I say. Is that why you're recording everything? So you can think about other stuff and not feel guilty because you can listen to it again later?

I can add in some commercial breaks if listening to me takes too much concentration, then you'll be able to switch off every now and then.

You're driving me crazy.

I mean, it's not like it's a difficult story to follow.

Anyway.

Baz never locks his door. That's just how he is. Otherwise, as he says, he's locked out when he forgets his keys. So whenever I feel like seeing him I go over to his place and wait.

I imagine that's how things will be when we live together. Once I even brought my toothbrush over and put it next to his.

I can't say he was super happy about it.

"I said you could only come if it was an emergency. What's the emergency?"

"I wanted to see you."

"Fine. But next time you get the urge, ring the bell, and if I'm not here you come back later. Is that clear?"

"But I like being with your things."

"Yeah, exactly. *My* things."

That was our first argument as a couple. Or about a couple thing anyway. Guys need freedom and all that. Jo was the one who warned me about that. Don't smother them too much or they'll freak out. And going to his place when he isn't there and waiting for him, or showing up while he's asleep in the night, well, apparently that's smothering.

I think it's cute, but hey.

So yeah. That's it.

The other night I was waiting at his place. But I was super proud of myself because I'd held back for ages. At least two days. I thought he was going to say he'd missed me, that he was worried, and all that stuff.

How stupid was I?

He came back with her.

He introduced the two of us. Like I gave a fuck about her name or what the fuck she does. She talked to me like I was an idiot. Like I was a kid. Any longer and she'd have been asking me what I wanted Santa to bring, and if I'd been a good girl.

Even though I'd waited two days so as not to smother him, he still wasn't happy. Two days!

And just so he could pick up another girl and then get angry when he came back to his house with her and shoved her in my face.

You don't do that to someone who brushes their teeth in your bathroom, right?

Fine, he hadn't said I could leave it there, but still. My toothbrush touched his while they were in the same glass. That counts, doesn't it?

Yeah, that counts.

I couldn't really speak while all this was going on. I was like a deer caught in headlights. Of an enormous fucking truck.

"Aicha, I've asked you not to just walk in like this. It really bothers me."

"But it's been two days…"

"Yeah… I thought you understood what I explained to you."

What he'd explained to me was crap. I didn't need to understand what he'd explained to me.

And anyway, I'd forgotten.

The slut said she had some things to do and she gave him a kiss on the lips to say goodbye.

Bang! The truck smashed me in the face.

Baz came to kneel down in front of me and told me not to cry. He said I just had to understand that it couldn't happen, me and him. That my feelings for him freaked him out, that he didn't want to know about anything happening between us, that he wasn't in love with me, that at the beginning he thought he could help me but now he was starting to see that the relationship was doing more harm than good blah blah blah.

I don't really remember what happened next, but I ended up back at home with my mother. That's what I was telling you about just now.

…

After that I went back to know for sure.

Why does he love me one day and the next he doesn't love me anymore? If it's just my age, then I'll get older, right. He can't not love me, it's not possible, we get along so well, he thinks I'm beautiful, he thinks I'm funny… What more do you need to love someone?

Nothing, right?

Everything was going well until that Élisanne Blais showed up on the scene.

…

Maybe it never happened, I thought. *Maybe I just dreamed it.*

When I came out of my room, my mother was adding the pasta to the water. As I left I heard her ask where I was going and tell me it would be ready soon. When I didn't reply, she shouted to ask if I'd be back before she left for work.

My mother's stupid. She thinks the more you shout, the more people listen.

But really people hear best when you whisper.

Through the door, I could hear Baz playing guitar. I listened for a few minutes and then went in without making a sound. I sat down next to him, but he didn't stop playing so I waited for him to finish the song.

I put my head on his shoulder. He sighed but didn't move.

"Do you love her more than me?" I asked.

"No, you know very well I don't."

"So why does she get to kiss you on the lips and I don't?"

He got up to put his guitar away, came back to the couch, and kissed me. On the lips.

It was a long meaningful kiss. Way better than the kiss Élisanne Blais got.

"You're the one I love. Not her."

…

When I came out of my room my mother was draining the pasta.

"It'll be ready in a minute. Sit down, I'll bring you a plate."

Truthfully, I went back to his place the next day. I couldn't hear his guitar so I knocked on the door when I arrived. Very quietly, like a little mouse.

But I'd been walking around for a while before I went there.

You know how sometimes when you walk everything falls into place? You make little movies and scenarios in your head... *He'll say this, I'll say that, and then this will happen. Or let's say he says something else, no big deal, I'll just pretend I didn't hear him.* Know what I mean? You go over all the possibilities in your head so you won't be surprised.

You know, like for example when he showed up with that ugly crazy cow, I didn't see it coming. If I'd seen it coming...

Yeah, no, I don't know.

So I walked. I don't know for how long. A long time. I wanted to walk down to the river. I could have pretended I was going to throw myself in... But if you want to get close enough to the river to do the big jump, you have to cross Notre Dame, and it's really dangerous with all the cars there. What if I got hit by a car while I was on my way to fake my own suicide... That would be pretty ironic, right?

. ˙ .

That's the kind of stupid thing that happens to me, so I didn't take any chances. I did another U-turn.

I seem annoyed, but actually I like irony. It irritates me but I like it. It's poetic.

It's like the South Shore: ugly and boring, and nobody wants to go there, but that's what you see when you look over there.

Which way's south anyway? Whatever. You know what I mean. And when you're there, in Brossard or wherever, looking at Montreal, you want to be there, it looks so beautiful you could cry, but you're not there.

That's ironic too. Complicated, cruel, tiring, but ironic.

Do you want me to carry on talking or do you want me to get back to when I went over to Baz's place?

So after I walked, I went back to Baz's place. And then I knocked really quietly. I basically just scratched at the door. He came and opened it and he seemed surprised. I looked up at him and bit my lip. The bottom one. I was giving it everything I had to look as cute as possible.

I didn't want it to seem like I'd come back for nothing, so I took off my sweater, his sweater that he'd lent me, and gave it back to him. I was wearing a tank top underneath. I swear he gave my breasts a quick look. Nothing much, not for long, just a glance.

A second, not even.

I hoped he wasn't comparing them to that bitch's. I was already regretting the sweater thing but it was too late.

"Since you don't want to see me anymore, I came to give this back," I said. Cute, pathetic, and half naked. If it had been raining, I would've been soaking wet too. He could have picked me up and frenched me, and then we could have made love.

He sighed and said, "Come in," and then, "Sit down."

I perched my ass right at the edge of the couch. As if I was about to leave. I didn't get comfortable because I didn't know what was going to happen. In all the scenarios I'd thought about while I was walking, I hadn't predicted this.

He went off on a long rant.

"I didn't mean to hurt you yesterday, Aicha. It's not that I don't want to see you anymore, I just need you to understand that…things are complicated. My feelings for you… I can't give you what you want. It can never happen. But it doesn't mean I don't like you, it doesn't mean I don't love spending time with you, it doesn't mean I don't think you're pretty. It's just…bad. I can't go there. Do you understand? Aicha, do you understand?"

I moved my head in a kind of nod-shake circle. Like I didn't know whether I understood or not.

He laughed.

He gave me his sweater back and I put it on.

"So is everything the way it was before? Nothing's changed?" I asked him.

He sighed and smiled at the same time, he sank down into the armchair and pulled me into him for a hug. He kissed me on the top of my head and said, "No. Nothing."

Everything went back to being perfect, the way it was before. For, I don't know, a week or two. Maybe three.

I tried to respect his freedom and what he was asking of me. We spent less time together but it was like quality time. We did some fun stuff. We watched movies, played guitar, cooked. We cooked stuff that was supposed to be better than mac and cheese with, like, gross mouldy cheese and vegetables that don't even really exist.

"Nothing's really changed at all," he told me.

You know what that's called?

A lie of omission.

Because that whole time, he was still seeing that woman, and doing stuff with her, and sleeping with her, and going over to her place and all that stuff. She was like his girlfriend or whatever.

They were seeing each other. And frenching each other. And screwing each other.

And he was touching her.

The fat fucking cow.

It's normal that I got mad when I found out, right?

No?

After everything he told me, after he said he loved me and all that stuff, what he wanted to do with me...

...

Yeah, he said that. I just told you that.

I thought everything was really gonna be like it was before, that she was gonna disappear and we'd never hear another word about her.

I didn't ever want to hear another word about her.

But that was no reason to do it behind my back, all that nasty stuff. I just thought she was going to get dumped or be removed from the picture or whatever, not that he was just gonna hide everything from me.

...

When you know something hurts someone you love, because he does love me, I know he does, then you don't do it. You don't just pretend you're not doing it. Don't take me for an idiot.

But I'm not mad at Baz. He didn't do it on purpose.

Well, I don't know.

What I do know is that it was her fault.

Love's pretty tiring, isn't it?

Yup.

And it was really stupid, the way I found out he was still seeing her.

Things had been going better with my mother. Since that evening I told you about before. She was less stupid for a while there. We even watched a chick flick together. Another time, we went clothes shopping and then out to eat. Like in a real restaurant. Not McDonalds. A restaurant that serves steak tartare and everything. I would've preferred McDonalds, but nothing's ever perfect, right?

We did a ton of stuff.

And when I wasn't doing stuff with her I was doing stuff with Baz. They were the busiest three weeks of my life. Even when nothing was going on I was busy thinking how good things were.

But like always, everything went wrong at the same time.

Yesterday evening my mother forgot her cellphone at home, on the living room table.

I looked through it, obviously. Seeing a phone lying around and not searching through it isn't human.

And what I found on it was totally gross.

Loads of texts between her and some guy. Phil. For weeks and weeks they'd been doing this whole relationship thing, texting *Goodnight* and *Thinking about you,* and she didn't want me to meet him because it would traumatize me, I was a difficult child, but happily we'd reconciled recently and she was sure she'd be able to tell me about him soon blah blah blah. And his two cents' worth: *I love you, I can't live without you anymore...* Fuck you! You're probably bald.

Anyway.

I don't like it when people lie to me and hide stuff from me.

So I went to see Baz. He's good at calming me down when I'm mad. And I also needed him to fix my mother's phone, which I'd accidentally thrown on the floor.

I tried to go in but the door was locked. The door's never locked. Ever.

I had a bad feeling. The seventh feminine sense. Or is it the sixth? How many senses are there, like four? I always get that mixed up.

Anyway, there was like a shiver up my spine.

She was the one who'd done that, locked the door so I couldn't get in, I felt sure. I was sure she was there.

You know how sometimes you just sense something?

Right then I could sense her.

Baz always leaves the balcony door unlocked too, just in case the front door gets locked. I seriously mocked him when he told me that. I loved him even more, but I laughed at him so he wouldn't be able to tell.

I went in through the window but he wasn't there.

She wasn't there either.

There was no one there. So I went back home and made myself some dinner.

That's the truth! I'm not lying!

I went back home and made myself a grilled cheese. And before that I had a shower.

…

Where is Baz? I'd like to see him. Does he know where I am?

I don't give a shit if he's been accused of murder! I've told you he didn't do anything! He wasn't even there.

I swear he didn't do anything.

He'd gone out to buy cigarettes at the convenience store. Or something or other at the grocery store.

…

I don't want to tell you about that now. Can we chat for a bit longer?

What else can we talk about? Is my mother coming?

…

I don't get why he's been accused. He's so cool he even likes cats.

This isn't what I wanted at all, I didn't think it through…

We love each other, do you get it? What's going to happen now? No, but seriously. What's going to happen?

Give me a glass of water and I'll tell you.

…

Thanks.

…

I didn't have a shower, and I didn't make myself a grilled cheese. We didn't have any orange cheese left, and anyway I wasn't hungry.

I turned on the new TV that my mother had bought but I wasn't really watching it. I was a bit dazed. Not really dazed, just totally beat. That whole day was totally surreal.

I didn't know if I'd dreamt it or what. I don't know if I wish I'd dreamt it.

The one time something happens in my life…

Baz came by and knocked on the door. That was weird because he'd never been to my place.

I didn't know if he was going to be mad or whatever, or just sad, or both.

As soon as he came in, he asked me what I'd done. There were smudges of dirt on him.

I replied, "It wasn't me, she was for real like that before I got there, I swear!" And I crossed my heart. To prove it to him.

He sighed. He took my hands in his, he like…examined them, and then looked at me like, *You want me to believe you with all this blood everywhere?*

It's true, I should've cleaned myself up. But when I got home I didn't have the strength left to do anything. I hurt all over, especially my arms. Look at the bruises I have there. And there.

"Why did you do it?" he asked.

Right then I didn't want to answer, I wanted to do the sulky girl thing. But I just told him the truth.

"Because you're mine."

He took me in his arms. His nose was in my hair. He was breathing so hard there was steam in my ear. He murmured, "I know, Aicha, I know."

You know, when the guy you love is crying, you're torn between wanting to take him in your arms, then apologize and tear out your organs one at a time to make him feel better, but at the same time, you're suddenly faced with the sad truth that yeah, he isn't actually invincible.

But that passes. And then you just want him to feel better.

You'd just like to go back in time and erase everything.

But you can't.

"I'm sorry, I didn't think you'd be so sad... Actually, I didn't think at all. But maybe she isn't dead. We could go back and see?"

But he said he didn't want me to go there again and that I should forget everything that happened.

"What everything?" I asked.

"Everything everything," he said.

"Everything?"

"Aicha, everything!"

That seems like a totally stupid conversation when I put it like that, but it was really intense at the time.

He helped me to wash. To clean up all the blood everywhere...

...

We made love, but it was sad. Not like the other times. He moved slowly and held me tight. I didn't like it.

I was just thinking of him and her.

I wondered if it was better with Élisanne Blais, seeing as she was more experienced and everything. I know people say that when you make love it's better if you actually, you know, love the person, but let's be clear: the bitch did have fucking great tits.

I'm sure he could do stuff with them.

"Did you do stuff with her tits?"

He didn't seem to understand, so I said it again. He said he'd understood fine the first time. I waited for his answer, but instead he just peeled himself off me, as if he was in pain, and made me promise I wouldn't forget what he'd told me.

"What are you going to do?" I asked. I don't promise anything without knowing what I'm promising. You shouldn't mess around with that. And you can see that I was right in the end. Look at the shit I'd be in if I'd promised him, am I right?

...

Yeah…no worse than I am now, is that what you're saying? Alright, so yeah.

He said I had to stay there. "If you love me, don't move," he said. "Don't say anything. Everything will be fine." Before he left I told him that I loved him. He sighed. And then he kissed me on the mouth.

I couldn't bear to watch him through my bedroom window as he walked away. I knew that nothing was gonna be alright.

I heard police sirens in the distance. I ran to ask Jo and Mel what was going on. They told me some guy had killed his girlfriend, it was a total bloodbath, thirteen stab wounds, we live in shitty times, he should be strung up by the balls, it could have been them, and on and on.

"No, it couldn't have been you," I said. And then I ran off.

There were police officers outside his building. They wanted to stop me getting through, but I shouted that I was the one who'd killed the girl.

They didn't believe me, they told me to get out of there. The bastards.

One of them came up to me and asked me how old I was and why I was out so late. I might have hit him a bit or insulted him, or maybe both. I can't remember too well.

They took me to the police station.

I told eight different people that it was me that killed her, not him. Nobody believes me. Why doesn't anyone believe me?

What's going to happen to him?

Is he gonna go to prison? Is he?

What's going to happen now?

…

You're not answering me.

I've told you everything and you're not answering me. You told me you could help me.

…

What does it change if he's admitted to it?

I say a lot of things too, and they aren't always true. I swear it was me, I swear. Write down that it was me. It's the truth, what I've told you, all of it, it's true.

Why did he say it was him? It wasn't him, I swear!

Can I see him?

Please!

…

I should've thought things through beforehand, but sometimes I lose it a bit.

…

What's going to happen to him?

Will he go to prison?

Why do only crap things happen in real life, and the fun stuff just happens in Hollywood or wherever? Don't bullshit me, tell me what's going to happen to him. I don't want him to go to prison, he can't go to prison, do you understand?

Do you understand?

Why did he say he did it?

…

If I tell you the truth, the *real* real truth, will he be okay?

…

That's the point of all this, right?

That's why I've been telling you my life story for...how long has it been? Four hours? Five?

All this stuff you're writing down—it means you're gonna tell them it wasn't him, right?

...

So...is that a yes? If I tell you the real truth, will he be fine? Okay.

I went back to his house and she was there. Sleeping in his bed. Naked. With her hair, her breasts.

It hurt me. Not just hurt a bit. It hurt like I might die of pain. You've never had pain like it. Nobody has. Ever.

I wanted it to stop. It had to stop.

Everything was spinning round in my head. So many pictures and sounds...

I wanted her to die.

There were loads of dirty dishes in the sink, but Baz always washes his knife right after using it and puts it back in the knife block. So it was easy to find.

And there you have it.

And he came to my house after...after.

Even now I don't know how he was feeling. He was crying, but sometimes you cry from anger or pain. Sometimes you might be sad, but not for the reason you ought to be sad.

He sat down on the living room couch.

He was shaking so much, he was so white it looked like he might break, or just disappear. It frightened me.

His cigarette ash fell on the carpet. I knew it would leave a mark and my mother would yell about it. Normally he would've cleaned it up, but right then I don't think he even realized there was a cigarette burning away in his hand.

"What have you done?" he said again.

I said, "I'm sorry," because I think it was a rhetorical question. You know, when someone asks you a question but it's not really a question.

He looked at me and he seemed so sad, like someone who's going to die and isn't very happy about it. I said I was sorry again. I said I didn't want him to be sad. I said I loved him and everything.

He started crying. He was shaking really hard, like a dying bird. His eyes looked even redder in his damp white face.

I had made him ugly.

"Why did you do it, Aicha? How could you do it?"

"I'm sorry… I'm sorry."

He had blood on his hands, on his jeans, and on his sweater sleeve. One of the stains looked a bit like a horse. A horse's head in profile.

I'm pretty good at describing stuff, but I could never manage to get across what his eyes were like. All the emotions in them. I don't have enough experience with eyes.

We stayed like that for a moment. He was staring into space like someone possessed. I was on the couch next to him but so far away I felt like I couldn't reach him even if I shouted.

I don't know how long we stayed like that. An hour…three days…a month. Maybe ten minutes. I don't know.

He sniffed, stood up suddenly, and said, "You need to wash your hands, have a shower, and get changed, okay?"

I just nodded my head.

Things had been moving fast, but now they were going so slowly that even his voice sounded deeper than normal.

"I threw your knife in the trash downstairs," I told him, while he was helping me clean the blood from under my nails.

He went down to get it while I had a shower. I wrapped myself up in a towel and I went back to him in the living room. He had the knife in his belt and my clothes in a bag.

"Are you going to wash them?"

"No, I'm going to throw them out. If anyone asks you, you were here all evening, all night. Don't say anything, okay?"

"Why? What are you going to do?"

"Aicha, this is important, what I'm telling you. Do you understand? Never tell anyone what happened. If you love me, you'll stay here and use all your twisted talents to tell stories and make everyone believe that you had no idea what was going on, okay? If you really love me, you're going to do what I tell you. Do you love me?"

"Yes, I love you, but what's going to happen?"

And I still hadn't promised, you noticed that, right? Write down in your notes that I didn't promise.

He didn't answer me, so I thought he was going to hit the road and take me somewhere cool to live, like Outremont, but on the beach. And with people who don't have sticks up their asses. Or better yet, with nobody. Just the two of us. A desert island just for us, like in James Bond, I can't remember which one. Do you know the one? The one with the blond woman?

I thought we were finally going to be together for real.

I still had drops of water all over my body, I hadn't dried myself. When he stroked me with his thumb, it made lines in the water. He rubbed me a bit to dry me. He was worried I was cold. "Your towel is soaked through," he said.

I took it off. He swallowed hard, and when he tried to look somewhere else, I leaned over and kissed him.

…

When I looked out of the window and watched him go, I was smiling.

I went back into the living room to write my mother a goodbye letter.

…

I didn't really know what to write in the damn letter. I'd already thought of a gazillion things that didn't want to come out right then. Not nice things, but…not mean things. I was so mad about that bald guy. But it was just like all those other times when my limbs decide for themselves what they want to do. Like my hand was refusing to move. So I let it do it.

Baz hadn't told me to pack a suitcase, but I still put Hakim's photo in my bag and packed my toothbrush and my cherry lip gloss.

I didn't want to look like a total train wreck and have sewer breath the first morning we for real woke up together, right?

In the movies people are always good-looking and they never smell. And it was a bit like a movie, what was going on with us. And it still is a bit, right?

Anyway. Then there were the sirens. I ran, I shouted…

You know the rest.

More or less.

…

Before he left, he didn't tell me where we'd be going. He didn't talk about a desert island or anything. Not even Outremont.

He just gave me a peck on the lips and said, "I love you too, Aicha. I love you too."